The First Time

The Fourteenth _ ...., ... y

From *New York Times* Bestselling Author

Jessica Beck

CUSTARD CRIME

Other Books by Jessica Beck

The Donut Mysteries

Glazed Murder
Fatally Frosted
Sinister Sprinkles
Evil Éclairs
Tragic Toppings
Killer Crullers
Drop Dead Chocolate
Powdered Peril
Illegally Iced
Deadly Donuts
Assault and Batter
Sweet Suspects
Deep Fried Homicide
Custard Crime

The Classic Diner Mysteries

A Chili Death
A Deadly Beef
A Killer Cake
A Baked Ham
A Bad Egg
A Real Pickle
A Burned Out Baker

The Ghost Cat Cozy Mysteries

Ghost Cat: Midnight Paws
Ghost Cat 2: Bid for Midnight

Jessica Beck is the *New York Times* Bestselling Author of the Donut Mysteries, the Classic Diner Mysteries, and the Ghost Cat Cozy Mysteries.

To you, my dear and treasured reader,
thanks for everything!

Custard Crime by Jessica Beck; Copyright © 2014

All rights reserved.

Chapter 1

Don't get me wrong; it's not as though it had never happened before. After all, murder had visited my family and friends often enough in our small town of April Springs, North Carolina, in the past. But when I got the news of just *who* had just died, I understood instantly that it would impact just about everyone in my life I knew and loved. Even given that, I still didn't realize just how bad things would ultimately get in the end.

It was a lot for a simple donutmaker to deal with, but then again, my life hadn't been all that easy since I'd first opened Donut Hearts, so why should this situation have been any different?

Chapter 2

"I can't believe this is our last walk together in the park," I said as I put my arm through Jake Bishop's and snuggled closer.

"Don't be so melodramatic, Suzanne," Jake, who also happened to be a state police inspector, said as he grinned down at me. "My month of physical rehab is up. We knew this day was coming from the very start." He flexed his right arm, the one where he'd been shot, and he didn't wince one little bit. "See? I'm as good as new."

"I still think you might be rushing things," I said. The truth was, I'd loved having Jake recover in my cottage, and I wasn't at all excited to see him go. It had nothing to do with the fact that I'd be living on my own. At least that was what I kept telling myself. Momma had finally gotten married and moved out of the cottage. She'd had almost a month to get used to her wedded bliss, and I had to say, it agreed with her. Our chief of police was one lucky man, and to his credit, he knew it better than anybody else did.

"Don't worry about me." Jake looked deep into my eyes, and it was clear that he could see something else was troubling me. That was one of the downsides to being with a state police inspector. He could read nuances like most folks read the newspaper, and I'd found it nearly impossible to deceive him. In a gentle voice, he said, "Hey, I know that it's going to be a big change for you once I'm gone, but your mother is close by, and Grace is just down the road. You won't be lacking for company, I can just about guarantee you that."

"I know you're right, but it still won't be the same without you here," I said. "It's been so nice having you downstairs."

He smiled warmly at me. "I've enjoyed it, too, but it's time for both of us to get back to work. You can't tell me that you don't miss it, too. After all, you've been away from the donut shop for as long as I've been here. A month is a long time not to do anything."

"Hey, I've been doing something very important," I said. "I've been taking care of you, not that you've needed it much lately."

"What can I say? I'm a quick healer," Jake said with a grin. "Anyway, I won't be gone all that long, and you know that I'll come back to April Springs every chance that I get. To be honest with you, I'm kind of surprised that you haven't gotten tired of me already."

I matched his smile with one of my own. "Right back at you, big guy," I said. "Do you really have to go today?"

"Sorry, but there's nothing I can do about it, Suzanne. I'm due in Raleigh at four," Jake said as he glanced at his watch. "That gives me three hours with you here in April Springs before I hit the road. What should we do in the meantime?"

I never had a chance to answer him, though, because that's when we heard the first siren that shattered the tranquility of our last day together for the foreseeable future.

Chapter 3

"What do you think is going on?" I asked Jake as we both stared as the fire truck came into view. "Do you smell smoke?"

He took a deep breath. "No, how about you?"

I did the same, and then I answered, "Nothing."

We started walking quickly through the park toward where the fire truck was parked, its siren now silenced but its lights still flashing brightly. It was the old building near Donut Hearts that had belonged to my mother until very recently, but I didn't know the woman who'd bought it from her very well.

"Look," Jake said as he pointed down the road. A police cruiser was racing to the scene, and an ambulance wasn't far behind. "That changes everything. Let's go see what's going on."

I resisted his pull, though. "You're not back on active duty yet, remember?"

He frowned for a moment before he spoke. "As a matter of fact, I was reinstated this morning over the phone."

This was news to me. "Where was I when all of this was happening?"

"You were upstairs in the shower," he said.

"Why didn't you tell me when I came down?"

He just shrugged. "I didn't want to spoil the day for either one of us, okay?"

"It's fine by me," I said. "If you're on the clock, though, that means that you probably should check out what's happening."

"Aren't you coming with me?" he asked me, clearly surprised by the possibility that I wouldn't tag along.

"Just try to stop me," I said with a grin. "I might not have any official status, but that doesn't mean that I'm not every bit as curious as you are about what's going on."

"Let's go, then," Jake said, and we both picked up our paces. It was a testament to his recovery that he was so ready to jump into action. I could still remember how fragile he'd been just after being shot, how much he'd slept in the days following the traumatic experience. This was a new man in front of me now, one that was ready and eager to leap back into danger. It was certainly a far cry from the fellow who'd hinted earlier that he might be done with law enforcement as a career. There was certainly no sign of that now, at least not that I could see.

"I'm right behind you," I said, and soon enough, we were both standing in front of the building.

Chief Martin was already there, conferring with the fire chief when we arrived. When he saw us, he nodded in our direction and held up a hand for us to wait.

"Stay right here," Jake said. "I'll be back soon."

"I'm going over there with you," I said.

"Suzanne, humor me, okay? The only way that either one of us is going to find anything out is if I act in my official capacity."

"Go on, then," I urged him, knowing that he was right. "I'll be waiting right here for you when you're finished."

"I'm counting on it."

After he was gone, I was tempted to wander the fifty yards across the tracks to the donut shop, but if I did that, I might miss out on what was going on where all the action was occurring, and that was something that I wasn't willing to risk. I'd be back at the helm the next day anyway, so it might not be a bad idea to enjoy my last day of freedom before I had to return to the daily grind of making donuts, not that I wasn't looking forward to it. Jake had been right about that, though I hadn't admitted it. I'd missed my work, and as much as it pained me to see him leave town, I was eager to get back to making donuts. I'd been creating dozens of recipes in my head and on paper since I'd been idle, and I couldn't wait to start trying some of them out. If one out of ten actually worked, I'd have a wonderful new selection to offer my customers very soon.

After a long conference between the fire chief, the police chief, and Jake, I watched as he broke away and headed back in my direction. "Sorry, but I'm afraid that I'm going to have to hang around and help out here for a while, Suzanne," he said.

I couldn't keep the disappointment from my face. "But you're not due to start work until later today, even if you have been reinstated."

"That may be true, but this situation is kind of delicate," he said softly.

"How so?"

"There's a dead body inside the shop," he replied, barely above a whisper.

Oh, no! "Who was it?" I asked.

"I can't say just yet, but I'll know more in a little bit," Jake replied, and then he headed inside the building, joined by the fire and police chiefs of April Springs.

I wasn't left alone, though, not by any means. There was quite a crowd gathering outside, including my assistant, Emma, and her mother, Sharon. They'd been running the donut shop for the last month while I'd tended to Jake, and we'd agreed to split the profits that had accrued under their tenure. I hadn't wanted to take any of it, but they'd both insisted, and in the end, I hadn't had much choice, not if I wanted to keep running my little donut shop for the foreseeable future.

Emma approached me as she asked, "What's going on, Suzanne?"

"I'm still waiting to find that out myself," I said.

Sharon joined us and said, "We were nearly out of donuts and we didn't have any customers at the moment, so we decided to lock the doors early and clean up after we find out what's going on. I hope you don't mind."

"Hey, it's still your shop today, so you can do whatever you please," I said with a smile.

"Suzanne, we all know that's not true. Donut Hearts will always be yours. My daughter and I have just been lucky enough to take over for the past month." She stifled a yawn and then added, "Though I won't mind sleeping in tomorrow the least little bit. I don't know how you've done it all these years."

"Always being a whisker away from bankruptcy has had a remarkable impact on my ability to get up every morning and make donuts," I answered with a smile.

Sharon nodded, and then she noticed someone drive up behind us. "If you'll excuse me, I'll go have a quick chat with my husband."

Ray Blake was not just another idle curiosity seeker there to see what was going on; he owned and ran the town's only newspaper, *The April Springs Sentinel*. It was mostly ads, but Ray prided himself on his journalistic abilities, so he was always searching for a titillating story for his front page. Even though I knew that we were dealing with a dead body here, I decided to keep that to myself. Let Ray discover that fact on his own. I didn't have anything against the man, but my first loyalty was to Jake, first, last, and always, and I was certain he wouldn't want me sharing what he'd just told me with the press.

"This is quite the scene, isn't it?" Emma asked as she looked around. "Should I go grab some coffee and the rest of our donuts to sell to the crowd?"

"My, aren't you the little entrepreneur," I said with a smile.

"Sorry, I've just gotten used to watching the bottom line all of the time. It's exhausting, isn't it?" she asked with a grin of her own.

I studied Emma closely before I spoke again. "Let me ask you something. Is it going to be demeaning for you to go back to just being my assistant tomorrow?"

"Are you kidding? I'm going to welcome it with open arms," she said, the relief clear in her voice. "Suzanne, I said it before, and I'll say it again. What you do every morning is more impressive than most folks can imagine. I'm actually looking forward to burying myself up to my arms in warm, sudsy water and letting my mind just wander. You're more than welcome to take things back over as far as I'm concerned."

"Thanks for saying that," I said.

I was about to add something to it when there was a commotion out front. Evidently something big was about to happen, and I didn't want to miss a moment of it.

Jake walked out of the building toward me, but that wasn't what caught my attention. Just behind him, Chief Martin looked as though he'd just been shot in the gut. His face was ashen, and it looked as though he was mere moments away from losing his lunch. I watched in surprise as Officer Grant steadied him, and when I glanced back at Jake, his grim expression triggered a flood of emotions in me.

"Did something happen to Momma?" I cried out, nearly collapsing onto the pavement.

Jake got there and managed to catch me before I could fall. "Take it easy, Suzanne. Your mother is fine."

"Are you sure?"

"I'm positive. As a matter of fact, I just spoke with her on the phone," he assured me. "She's on her way."

"If Momma's okay, then what's wrong with the chief? He looks as though he's just seen a ghost."

In a softened voice, Jake said, "He's pretty shook up, but then he has a right to be. The body they found inside was his ex-wife."

"Evelyn is dead?" I asked in disbelief. I had never been a big fan of the woman after the trouble she'd once made for my mother, but I certainly hadn't wished her that much ill. "What happened to her?"

"At first glance, it appears to have been an accident,"

Jake said carefully.

"But you don't believe that, do you?" I asked as I studied him closely. Maybe I'd learned to read him as well since we'd been together.

He shook his head. "Not a chance. It looks staged to me. I hate to do this, but I'm going to have to call my boss. There's no way that the chief is going to be able to investigate this himself."

"Are you going to do it?" I asked him. "That would be perfect. After all, you're already here, and besides, you know just about everyone in town."

Jake shook his head wearily. "Suzanne, that's precisely why I'm the *worst* person to investigate this murder. I have too many opinions and prejudices about this case before it even begins, and more ties to the people involved than any investigator should have."

"But don't you see? That's what could be your most powerful asset." Not only did I want Jake to stay and take over because he was the best man for the job, but if he were to take it, that would mean that I wouldn't have to say good-bye to him quite so soon.

"I don't have time for this conversation right now," Jake said as he pulled out his phone. "I just wanted to let you know what was going on."

I hadn't even seen Ray Blake standing nearby, which was the newspaperman's intention, I was sure. He'd been lurking and eavesdropping in on our conversation, and when he'd gotten all that he could out of Jake that way, he decided to try a more direct way to question him. "Inspector, I understand that the victim was Evelyn Martin, Chief Martin's ex-wife. Would you care to comment?"

Jake gave the reporter an icy glare that shook me a little in its intensity. I was seeing the cold side of him at that moment, the professional lawman that didn't put up with any interference from outsiders. After staring at Ray for a full ten seconds, he finally just grunted, "No comment."

"Surely you have something to say," Ray pressed him.

"Off the record?" Jake asked, surprising me and the newspaperman.

"Sure thing," Ray replied eagerly.

Jake took a step closer, now looming over him. "If you don't hold this until tomorrow, you'll never get another useful thing out of me for as long as I'm around, and I plan on being here for a very long time."

I had to give Ray credit. He didn't even flinch. "And if I choose to cooperate, what do I get then?"

"My respect, and a shot at some cooperation later on down the line," Jake said.

Ray shook his head. "Sorry, but I only deal in things that I can write about. I don't care how you feel about me. That's not my job."

"Then we're through," he said.

Emma's father just shrugged as he made his way out into the growing crowd.

"Sorry about that," I told Jake.

"It's not your fault," he replied curtly. "I should have been paying closer attention to who was around us."

"That's because of me, though. Ray wouldn't have overheard you if you hadn't been updating me on what was going on."

Jake shook his head. "Suzanne, you didn't run and tell him what I shared with you, so I'm not about to blame you. Now, if you'll excuse me, I really do need to go make that call now." He was a little brusque with me as he said it, but that could have just been a part of him doing his job. At least that's what I hoped it was. As Jake stepped aside to have a little privacy, I saw Momma finally show up on the scene. She headed straight for the chief the moment she arrived, and when she got to him, Officer Grant quietly peeled away and went back to stand guard in front of the empty shop. We'd run Momma's truncated mayoral campaign out of that building, and I had been pleased for her when I discovered that she was finally selling it to Beatrice Ashe. That still didn't tell me what Evelyn Martin had been doing inside, though. I knew that Beatrice and Evelyn were friends, forming a kind of alliance after both had been divorced at about the same time, but that didn't explain her presence in the building.

I heard Jake raise his voice, so I glanced over in his direction and saw him arguing with someone over the phone, most likely his boss. What did that mean? I didn't have to wait long to find out. He rejoined me less than a minute later, and he clearly wasn't happy about the outcome of the conversation.

"Well, be careful what you wish for, Suzanne, because it might just come true," Jake said unhappily.

"Does that mean that you got the job?"

"I tried to talk him out of it, but my boss saw it the same way that you did. I know the players involved, so he thinks I'll have more of a chance to wrap it up quickly. I think there's more to this than meets the eye, though."

"How so?" I asked, trying to contain my enthusiasm for his continued presence. I hated the reason for it, but nonetheless, Jake was going to be hanging around a little longer than either of us had anticipated, and that was the sliver of silver lining in the black cloud of Evelyn Martin's death.

"He's clearly not sure that I'm ready to hit the ground running when I get back to Raleigh, so he's giving me an easy one to start off with so that I can work myself back into active duty."

"Do you think this case is going to be that simple to solve?" I asked him.

"I can't say that one way or the other just yet, but most likely it's not in the same league as tracking down mad dogs and serial killers," Jake said. He frowned as he added, "Whoever tried to stage this clearly wasn't a professional."

"How so?" I asked him. I clearly wanted more details than he was willing to give.

"I can't talk about it right now, Suzanne," he said as he headed over to where Momma and Chief Martin were in deep conversation. I watched as Jake gave the chief the news. After he told him, Jake dialed a number on his phone and then handed it to the police chief. It was no doubt direct orders from his boss. I watched the chief's expression as he listened, but all he did was nod, and then he handed the phone back to Jake. Momma pulled Chief Martin away, and Jake reentered the building, making sure to speak with Officer Grant on his way inside. The young officer nodded, and then repositioned himself in front of the building. It was clear that no one was getting in without permission, and sadly, that included me.

For the moment, there was nothing that I, or anyone else standing vigil outside, could do.

"I'm sorry about Dad," Emma said a minute later as she rejoined me. "You know how he gets when he has the slightest whiff of a story."

"I'm not the one who has a problem with him."

"That's a relief," Emma said with a happy sigh.

"I wouldn't be too joyous about that just yet. Jake was pretty upset, and believe me, he's one man you don't want to have against you."

"Doesn't he know that Dad was just doing his job?" Emma asked plaintively.

I knew that I couldn't win if I let this conversation continue. If I took Jake's side, which I was inclined to do for many reasons, it would just alienate Emma, but if by some bizarre reasoning I defended Ray's position, it would put me in direct opposition of the man I loved. "Tell you what. Let's just agree not to discuss this situation anymore. How does that sound?"

"Sorry. You're right," Emma said apologetically. "So, you're still coming back to Donut Hearts tomorrow, right?"

"Just try to keep me away," I said. "Could you do me a favor and ask your mother to come by the shop after we close tomorrow?"

Emma frowned. "Why? What's wrong?"

"Not a thing. I'm going to go over the books tonight, so I'd like to pay the two of you your share of the profits for the past month as soon as possible."

"There's no hurry," Emma said, clearly happy that nothing else was wrong.

"Emma, you should know me well enough by now to realize that I always pay off my debts as soon as I possibly can," I told her. "I'm going by the shop this afternoon to collect all of the reports and deposit slips for the last thirty days, and I'll have a figure for you tomorrow."

"Why don't I grab them for you now?" Emma asked a little too eagerly.

What was going on? "Emma, is there something at Donut Hearts that you don't want me to see?"

"The place is a mess," she confessed. "We haven't had a chance to clean up for the day yet, and I don't want you to see it the way that it is right now. Let me grab the books for you, Suzanne. Please?"

"I suppose that's all right," I said. "Just make sure that the place is in good shape before you go. I want a clean start tomorrow when I come back."

"Understood. I'll just be a few minutes," she said, and after grabbing her mother, Emma took off down the road back to Donut Hearts.

How bad must the place be if she was that reluctant to let me see it? I was tempted to follow the mother and daughter back to the shop, but that wouldn't do anyone any good. I'd given Emma and Sharon time to clean things up, so it would be doing them a disservice peeking in now, no matter how much I wanted to.

As good as her word, Emma found me five minutes later as I stood vigil waiting for something else to happen in front of the crime scene.

My assistant shoved the last month's worth of receipts into my hands.

"Does this include everything?" I asked.

"Right up to today's receipts," she said.

"Then I'll work on this today and let you know where things stand tomorrow," I said.

"Like I said, there's no hurry."

"Nevertheless, we'll take care of this tomorrow." I had a sudden thought. "If your mother would like, we could even do this *before* work tomorrow."

Emma smiled, and then she said, "Thanks, but you heard her before. I think she's looking forward to sleeping in tomorrow morning."

"I can't blame her for that a bit." I myself still hadn't really gotten used to my later waking hour, but ironically, I'd just started to adapt when it was time to go back to my former schedule of getting up when anyone in their right mind would still be sound asleep.

"Well, I'd better get back to the shop and finish cleaning up," Emma said. "Suzanne, I'll see you bright and early tomorrow morning."

"I'm looking forward to it," I said, and I realized as I said it that it was true. Getting back to the daily routine at the donut shop was exactly what I needed. My life had been a little rudderless in my time away, so it would be wonderful to get back to work.

I just hoped that Jake felt the same way, now that he was officially responsible for finding Evelyn Martin's murderer.

Chapter 4

I realized that Grace must have still been at work as I walked past her place and saw that her driveway was empty, so I decided to head straight to the cottage and get started on the Donut Heart receipts. At least my place would be quiet. As a matter of fact, it would probably be a little *too* quiet with Momma and Jake both gone, so I decided to turn on the radio when I got home. I finally managed to find a broadcast of soft rock that served as a perfect buffer to the silence. After that, I made myself a cup of tea, and then I spread everything out on the kitchen table and organized the reports for every day of the month that I'd been absent from Donut Hearts. After studying each individual report from the register, my hunch was that they didn't do too badly at all while I'd been gone. I went through the totals a little more thoroughly the second time around, and then I figured out what my average daily expenses were. I knew this number fairly well already, so it was easy to calculate just how much profit I'd be splitting with Emma and her mother. I knew better than anyone the razor-thin profit margins I worked with at the donut shop, and I hoped that Emma and Sharon would realize that I was doing the best that I could when I wrote their checks. I considered padding the amount that I owed them for one second, but then I realized that I wouldn't be doing anyone any favors if I did that. In the end, I wrote out a statement that showed the donut shop's income for the past thirty days, deducted the expenses, and then I tallied the final profit. After splitting that in half, I split their share again and wrote one check for Emma and another one for her mother. It had taken us some time to work out the details, since Emma usually drew a salary from me independent of sales. My assistant came out ahead running the shop for a month, but not by much. It was clear that she would have been better off with things the way they usually were, earning a little less money in exchange for a great many fewer headaches. I wasn't looking forward to having that particular conversation with her the next morning, but it turned out that I didn't have to wait that long after all. The ink on both checks was barely dry when there was a knock on my front door.

"Hey," I said as I opened it and saw Emma and Sharon standing at my doorstep. "I thought we were getting together tomorrow after work."

"We decided that we needed to talk about the split before then," Sharon said gravely.

Oh, no. Were they going to ask for a bigger cut? I could probably live with it, but it was going to seriously hamper my ability to run the business for the next few weeks.

"Come on in," I said as I stepped aside, putting on as brave a face as I could manage, given the circumstances. "I just had a cup of tea, but I'd love to join you in another if you're interested."

"There's no need to do that. This won't take that long," Sharon said.

"Mother, I'm still not sure that we should—" Emma said before her mother cut her off.

"Emma, I've made up my mind." She then turned to me and said, "Suzanne, we need to have a serious discussion about our earlier arrangement."

"Would you at least like to sit down?" I offered.

"That won't be necessary. We don't want to take up too much of your time," Sharon said.

"But we'd love to sit down and relax while we're here," Emma insisted, plopping herself down onto my sofa despite her mother's refusal.

"Now, what exactly did you have in mind?" I asked Sharon after they were both settled in on the couch. "There's no reason that this has to be tense. I'm open to any reasonable request you might have. After all, you both did me a huge favor keeping Donut Hearts open while I took care of Jake."

"It was fun," Sharon said, "but ultimately, the donut shop is a business, so we need to be businesslike when we discuss this. Suzanne, Emma and I have given this a great deal of thought, and we've decided that the percentage split you've offered isn't entirely fair."

Ouch. I'd be lying if I didn't say that stung a little. "To be fair, I tried to talk you both out of splitting the profits with me fifty-fifty from the very start, but you insisted. It's fine if you want a bigger share now. I understand completely. What did you have in mind?"

Sharon looked at me oddly, and then she smiled. "Is *that* why you think we're here? Suzanne, we don't want more, my dear; we're asking for less. All we did was keep the shop open in your absence; you're the one who built it from nothing. Fifty percent of your profits is too much, not too little. Would you settle on keeping two thirds of the profits for yourself and letting my daughter and me split the remaining third?"

"I would not," I said sternly. "Ladies, a deal is a deal. When you see the small amount that you both actually earned, you might reconsider your kindness altogether."

"Whatever you can spare is fine with us," Sharon said. "Right, Emma?"

"Don't look at me," my assistant said. "I told you how Suzanne would react, and I agree with her one hundred percent. We made a deal to split the profits right down the middle, and it's not fair to try to change that now, in either direction."

I laughed at Emma's insistence, knowing that I would have done the exact same thing if our roles had been reversed.

"What's so funny?" she asked me.

"I don't know which one of us should be more proud of you, me or your mother," I replied as I stood. "Let me grab your checks, since you're already here."

I went into the kitchen and collected both checks, as well as the statement I'd made out as an explanation. As I handed each woman her earnings for the month, I said, "Here's the breakdown, if you'd care to see it."

"That won't be necessary. We trust you," Sharon said even as Emma was reaching for the sheet.

"Remember, we need to trust, but always verify, Mom," she said with a smile. After studying the document for a minute, Emma said, "Suzanne, this isn't right."

I looked at the sheet and studied it for a few seconds. "What's wrong with it? It looks fine to me."

"Our daily expenses were a little higher than this while you were gone."

"How could you possibly know that?" I asked her.

Emma admitted, "I'm taking a business accounting class at my community college, so I put everything into a spreadsheet so we could track our expenses better." She paused a moment before adding, "I hope you don't mind."

"Mind? I think that it's terrific," I said. "But keep the checks I wrote you. It can't be a big enough difference to make up for the hassle for me to rewrite them."

"Okay," Emma said. "Thank you."

"I'm just sorry that it's not more," I said. "But then again, that's the business that I'm in."

"That *we're* in," Emma said, stressing the fact that we were in it together. "Don't worry. I warned Mom that it probably wouldn't even be this much."

"I don't know what you two are talking about. I'm delighted to add this much to my travel budget," Sharon said. She'd developed a taste for Europe lately, and since her husband was married to his newspaper as much as he was to Sharon, she'd found a female friend who loved to travel as much as she did. In the end, everyone had been delighted with the arrangement, none more than Ray Blake, though I suspected that Sharon was a close second.

"Now, are you sure that I can't get you something to drink?" I asked.

"No, we've got some things to do, but thank you," Sharon said.

"The first place on our list is the bank," Emma said with a grin. "I've been living on savings this past month."

"You haven't missed any meals, young lady," Sharon answered with a smile. "As a matter of fact, it's been nice having you eat at home with your father and me."

"Well, get used to seeing me gone again, because I'm planning to eat out the rest of the week."

After I saw the two women off, I pondered just how lucky I was to have such good friends around me. Sharon and Emma were just the beginning. Nearly everyone who even remotely touched my life had helped out one way or another when I'd been taking care of Jake, and I appreciated every last one of them. I wished that there was some way I could repay each and every person, but the task would have been too daunting. In the end, all that I could do was to make sure that whenever any of them needed me, I was there for them. And honestly, that was the best way to repay their kindness, anyway.

With that straightened out, I decided to fix myself a little something to eat, since there was no telling when Jake would make it back to the cottage. I was just about to take out the last of a ham someone had brought over when I saw a police cruiser pull up outside.

Oh no! Had something else happened?

And more importantly, was Jake safe?

Chapter 5

I needn't have worried. It quickly turned out to be Jake, currently driving a car from the April Springs Police Department.

As I went out onto the porch, I said, "That's one sweet ride you've got there, mister."

He shrugged. "They insisted that I drive it, and I got tired of fighting them, since I don't have a car at the moment. If you'll remember, you're the one who drove me here in the first place."

"I'm not likely to forget that," I said, remembering the ride home from the hospital in Hickory. It had been almost exactly one month ago, and in many ways, my time at the cottage with Jake had flown by. Discounting a few run-ins with the criminal element along the way, we'd had a fine time of it as he'd recovered.

"Are you hungry? Because I'm starving," Jake asked.

"I was just about to make something," I replied. "I can do it for two just as easily as one."

"Tell you what. Why don't we skip that, as tempting as it sounds, and go grab a bite at the Boxcar?"

"You don't have to ask me twice," I said as I closed the cottage door behind me and locked it. "It's a beautiful afternoon. Let's walk through the park, shall we?"

"Suzanne, are you *still* trying to get me to exercise?" Jake asked me with a smile that I'd grown to love even more over the past month.

"No, that's just a bonus. The truth is I don't want to be seen riding around in that squad car."

"We could always take your Jeep," he suggested.

"No, let's walk. Besides, it will give us a chance to chat."

"Why don't I like the sound of that?" he asked.

"Maybe it's because you're just a typical suspicious man," I replied with a slight smile.

"I don't know. In all the times in the past that a woman has told me that we needed to talk, it's never turned out well for me."

"So, maybe it's time to turn your luck around," I said as I took his hand in mine.

"Is it, though?" he asked me, still rather doubtfully.

"No, not so much," I admitted with a wry grin.

After a deep sigh, Jake said, "That's what I suspected. Go on. Let's get it over with. Tell me what's on your mind."

"Gee, what a lovely attitude that is," I said. "It's really not *that* bad."

"I'll believe that when I hear what you have to say," Jake said.

"The truth is that I'm just curious about what really happened today," I said, trying to sound as nonchalant as I could manage.

"I'm afraid that I can't tell you anything about that. After all, it is official police business," Jake said.

"Really?" I asked as I stopped dead in my tracks. "You can't even give me a hint about where things stand right now?"

"I'm really not supposed to do even that," Jake said. "Surely you understand."

"What I understand is that you're not going to satisfy my idle curiosity. It's not like you're under some kind of doctor-patient confidentiality agreement, or an attorney's vow of silence, either. Chief Martin has even shared things with me over the last several months."

Jake frowned. "Well then, the two of us must conduct police business in different ways."

"What if I promise to keep anything that you tell me confidential?" I asked him suddenly.

He laughed at the suggestion. "Suzanne, I wouldn't dream of putting you in that kind of bind. Telling you and not allowing you to say anything to Grace or your mother would just be cruel."

"Not if I'm volunteering for it," I protested. "After all, I can keep a secret just as well as the next person."

"I don't doubt that, but why put yourself through it if you don't have to?"

"Because I really want to know what happened to Evelyn Martin," I said simply.

Jake and I started walking again, and after a full minute of silence, he finally said, "Well, it's against my better judgment, but if you give me your word that you won't share what I'm about to tell you with anyone else, I suppose I could make an exception this once."

"You won't regret it," I said eagerly. "Now, tell me everything."

Jake nodded as he steered us toward one of the benches in the park between my cottage and Trish's diner. "Why are we sitting down? Are you tired?" I asked him.

"No, I'm fine. I just don't want to share what I'm about to tell you in that crowded diner."

"Good plan," I said as we sat. "Don't leave a single thing out from when we first split up at the crime scene. How did you know that it was a crime scene, by the way?"

"Well, the body was a good initial indicator," Jake said with a slight smile.

"That's not necessarily true. People have accidents all the time," I said.

"And that's what the killer was trying to make us all believe this time," Jake said. "Now, am I going to tell this before we both starve to death, or are you going to keep interrupting me?"

"I'll be quiet," I said, and then I added quickly, "Let me rephrase that. I'll try to be quiet."

"Knowing you, I'll take what I can get," Jake said with the hint of a grin that vanished just as quickly as it had appeared. "Suzanne, thirty seconds after I walked into that building, I knew that it was murder, and no accident."

"How did you manage to learn that?" I asked.

"For starters, it just didn't feel right to me from the start," Jake said. "I've seen enough real murders to be able to spot them right away, even if someone has tried to cover their tracks."

This was fascinating information. "How did you know in this case?"

Jake scratched his chin, and then he said, "First of all, the body was positioned all wrong. If she'd *fallen* through the loosened floorboards, she would have hit the basement floor farther away from the wall, based on where the hole was situated upstairs. I knew right away that she'd probably been pushed. And then there was the candle next to her body."

"What about it? Was it still burning when they found her?" For some reason, that image really unsettled me.

"No, it had been lit for only a few seconds, based on the amount of wick that was touched by flame. There was no way the victim was using it to see inside the building. The third indicator was that there was direct evidence of a purposeful blow to the head. From the sharp indentation on the back of her skull, something with a hard ninety-degree edge was used to kill her."

"Is that how she died, by blunt force trauma?" I asked.

"That was how it looked to me from the start, but the odd thing was that none of the exposed joists where she must have fallen had any signs of blood or hair on them, so we know that she didn't hit her head on any of them, and the floor itself was flat. As a matter of fact, there were no objects within reach that could have caused her wound, so the murder weapon had to have been removed from the shop *after* the crime was committed. We didn't discover the final interesting fact until we searched the floor of the basement and the body."

"What was that?"

"There was no sign of matches or a lighter anywhere around Evelyn or on her person," Jake said.

"So she couldn't have lit the candle herself," I added.

"Bingo. Add it all up, and this was murder, plain and simple. When I pointed these things out to my boss, he insisted that I take over the case. We both realized that someone from outside April Springs had to investigate this as soon as I told him what I'd found."

"Why was that, just because the victim was the police chief's ex-wife?"

Jake nodded. "Even the appearance of impropriety is enough to call for an outside investigator. I just wish that it wasn't me."

"Don't worry. I'm sure that you'll catch the killer in record time," I said.

"We'll see," he said as he rubbed his chin thoughtfully. "Remember, you can't share what I've just told you with anyone. Suzanne, you're going to keep that promise, right?"

"Jake, I gave you my word," I said, but then I realized just how hard it was going to be to keep what I knew from my mother and Grace, along with everyone else in April Springs. "Maybe this wasn't such a good idea after all."

"That's what I kept telling you," he said, "but I'm afraid that we're stuck with me investigating the murder now."

"I don't mean that. I still think that it's brilliant that you're looking into Evelyn's murder. I'm just not sure that I need full disclosure from you about your investigation."

"I thought you might feel that way after you heard what I'd found so far. Suzanne, you and Grace aren't going to dig into this case too, are you?"

"Why shouldn't we?" I asked, surprised that he'd even had to ask. "We could be of great service to you in your investigation, you know."

Jake took in a deep breath, held it for a beat, and then slowly let it out before he trusted himself to speak. "The chief might have put up with your meddling, but I shouldn't have to remind you that I'm not Chief Martin."

"No, I know that clearly enough. But think about it, Jake. Grace and I could both really be assets for you. No one doubts your abilities as a law enforcement officer, but we'll be able to get folks to chat with us unofficially in ways that they'd never do with you."

"I understand that," Jake conceded. "I just don't want to put myself into a position where I have to arrest my girlfriend for obstruction of justice."

"Oh, you don't have to worry about that," I said as I pulled him to his feet.

"Because you're going to leave this case to me and my temporary police force?" Jake asked.

I laughed, and then I said, "I'm not saying that at all. We just won't be clumsy enough to get caught doing anything you think we shouldn't be doing."

"Why am I not relieved to hear you say that?" Jake asked as we neared the diner.

"You should be. Just think about what a team we'll all make."

"Suzanne, I'd rather not, if it's all the same to you. Chief Martin has already been making noises that he wants to be involved in the case, and I've had to tell him no pretty forcefully. How is he going to feel if he finds out that I've given you and your best friend access that I won't allow him to have?"

"I'm sure that he'll understand, once Momma explains it to him," I said.

"I don't doubt that your mother's powers of persuasion are strong, but even she is not that convincing."

"You don't give her enough credit. The chief will see that what we're all doing is in his best interest. I can just about guarantee that."

"Suzanne, I'm still not sure that I'm willing to go along with you and Grace investigating a case that I'm actively working on myself."

"That's okay. Take some time and get used to it if you need to," I said happily.

"Is that my only choice?" Jake asked me glumly.

"Let's not talk about it right now," I said as we got to the front steps of the Boxcar. "After all, your original point was a good one. It won't do anyone any good if folks hear all of the details about what really happened to Evelyn."

"Given April Springs, I'm sure that it won't be long until the true story is spread from city limit sign to city limit sign."

"What can I say? Gossip is an Olympic event around here," I answered as I led him up the stairs and inside.

Fortunately, Jake didn't have time to reply as a crowd of citizens approached him all at once, each of them shouting different questions about what really happened to Evelyn Martin, and who exactly might have done it.

Fortunately, Trish stepped in before things got too ugly.

"Settle down, people," she said loudly, but no one seemed to listen to her. That changed the moment she slammed a baseball bat down onto the counter that held the cash register. That certainly shut everyone up fast enough. Once her customers were quiet enough to satisfy Trish, the diner owner said loudly, "I'm sure the inspector appreciates your questions and your concerns, but this isn't a press conference, and we're not standing out in front of the town hall. I'm guessing the man and his girlfriend have come here to eat, and so help me, if anyone interferes with that happening even the least little bit, they'll have to answer to me. Is that clear?"

There might have been a few grumbles, but no one was insane enough to voice them out loud.

Trish smiled, and then she said, "Now, go back to your meals, or bring your checks up to the front and I'll cash you out. This mob is officially disbanded as of right now."

Folks began to do as she'd suggested—ordered, really—and Trish smiled as she walked over to us. "I've got a table near the front and one in back. Take your pick."

"Let's go to the back," I said, and Trish nodded in agreement.

"Smart idea. That will keep the riffraff from 'dropping by' your table on their way out the door. Hang on. I'll be with you in a second."

"Thanks," Jake said as he smiled down at Trish.

"You're welcome. After all, you need to eat, too."

"Honestly, I'm starving," Jake said, "but your cooking has put five pounds on me in the month I've been in April Springs healing up."

"You can't blame that all on me," she answered with a smile. "I've seen the parade of pasta, cakes, and pies that have made their way to your doorstep since you came to town. I've got a hunch that my contributions are the least of it."

"I'd never call your food the least of anything," Jake said with a smile.

Instead of responding to him, Trish turned to me. "You know, this one might just be a keeper."

"That's the direction that I'm leaning myself, but it's still too soon to say just yet," I answered her with a smile.

"Well, make up your mind before too long. There might be other women around here who could possibly be interested in having a state police inspector of their own." Trish winked at Jake as she said the last bit, and he managed to blush a little.

"Sorry I can't be more accommodating, but this one's all mine," I said as I put my arm in his.

"Hey, I'm still sitting right here, remember?" Jake asked.

"Nobody's about to forget that," Trish said. "You two figure out what you'd like to eat and I'll be with you in a shake. Two sweet teas to start?"

I looked at Jake, who nodded happily. "That sounds great, but don't give either one of us refills, no matter how much we beg for them."

"Suzanne, that's just inhumane," Trish said with a grin, "but I understand."

Once we were left alone to study our menus, I thought that we'd be free to enjoy a meal together without interruption.

But then again, I hadn't counted on Gabby Williams marching up to our table, either.

Evidently she wasn't the least bit afraid of Trish's warning.

Then again, I wasn't sure who I'd put my money on if Trish and Gabby ever decided to fight it out. Trish was young and scrappy, but Gabby had a will of iron, and a tongue that could cut through flesh with its barbs. Either way, if it ever did occur, I didn't want to be within a country mile of it.

Chapter 6

"Hello, Gabby. I don't know if you just heard Trish or not, but you should understand that Jake and I are here to grab a bite to eat and have a little privacy." I'd learned years before that Gabby didn't understand subtlety. She ran the shop next to mine, ReNEWed, a place where folks could get gently used clothing for a decent price. Gabby was also the biggest gossipmonger in four counties, as well as being civilly acidic in just about every social situation.

"I don't blame you one single bit," Gabby said as she sat down across from us. As she looked around the diner, she added, "They can be a real pain sometimes, can't they?" She then turned to stare at Jake for a full ten seconds before she said, "I understand that you're in charge of finding Evelyn Martin's killer."

"That's right," Jake said.

"Have you made any progress yet?"

Jake looked a little surprised by how abrupt she was. "I'm not at liberty to discuss that."

Gabby grinned. "Sure, I get it. In cop-speak, that means you've got nothing. Well, this is your lucky day, Inspector. I've got not one, but two hot leads for you."

"I'm always happy to listen to information from concerned citizens," Jake said in a calm, level voice.

I tried to warn him off from encouraging her, but he must have missed my signal. I knew that Gabby might indeed have valuable information for the investigation, but if she started talking now, our meal would be ruined. Besides, it wasn't as though she wouldn't share it with us later, especially if it was too good for her to keep to herself for very long.

"Okay, then maybe you should get out your pencil and paper and take notes," Gabby said. "First off, you need to look at Robby Chastain, and I mean hard."

"Robby? Are you sure?" I asked her. I couldn't imagine anyone naming Robby a murder suspect. I'd known the man nearly my entire life, and I couldn't see him killing anyone.

Gabby iced me with a quick glance. "Suzanne, if you'd take your head out of your donuts for a minute or two, you'd know that Robby and Evelyn were in the middle of a battle over an oak tree on their property line. Robby's been wanting to cut that thing down for years, but Evelyn told him if he tried it, she'd burn his house to the ground in retaliation."

"That sounds like a bit of an overreaction on her part," Jake said.

"You didn't know Evelyn. She always was fire and ice."

"What do you mean by that?" he asked her.

"Either you were her best friend in the world, or you were her greatest enemy. There was no in-between with that woman."

"May I ask, how did she feel about you?" Jake asked her.

"We were best buds," Gabby said. "Why else do you think I'm trying to help you find her killer?"

"He probably just thought that you were a concerned citizen," I said with a smile that I knew was pushing my luck, but I didn't care. After all, she was interrupting my time with Jake with what I suspected were overblown exaggerations and innuendoes.

Gabby waved a hand in the air in my direction as if dismissing me from the conversation. "We both know better than that. Anyway, it wouldn't surprise me if Robby got tired of Evelyn's insults and decided to eliminate her altogether."

"All of this over a tree?" Jake asked incredulously.

"Oh, there had been more things than that between them over the years. The tree was just the final tipping point."

"Can you be more specific about their past interactions?" Jake asked her.

"Inspector, I'm not going to do your *entire* job for you," Gabby said disdainfully.

I noticed that Trish had started to walk toward us, but when she saw Gabby sitting with us, she did a quick U-turn and headed back to the register. There weren't many folks in town that could back the Boxcar owner down, but Gabby was evidently one of them. Great. Now we were never going to get to eat.

"You said that you had two leads to share with me," Jake reminded her.

"Don't get your undies in a knot," Gabby said. "I'm getting to that. The second person you need to look at is Julie Gray."

"I don't know her," I said. "She doesn't live in April Springs, does she?"

"Union Square," Gabby said.

"What does she have to do with Evelyn's murder?" Jake asked her.

"You didn't know?" Gabby asked, feigning surprise. "She's Evelyn's second cousin."

"And how exactly is that relevant to the investigation?" Jake asked her.

"From what Evelyn told me, Julie was her closest living relative, and unless she changed her mind in the last few days before she died, I got the distinct impression that Julie was set to inherit everything that Evelyn had."

"Is that very substantial?" I asked. "I thought that Evelyn was pretty much broke."

"Oh, she had money, and I'm talking serious cash," Gabby said. "She just didn't want anyone in town to know about it."

"Was Chief Martin even aware of it?" I asked.

"No, this all happened after they split. Evelyn inherited five hundred thousand dollars from her great aunt last month, and the kicker was that Julie didn't get a dime of it in the old lady's will. She resented Evelyn for it, and she didn't mind who knew it. If she's the one who did it, it wasn't just so she could get Evelyn's meager possessions. She wanted the bigger prize of all that money Evelyn had just gotten herself."

"I'll look into both of your tips," Jake said, and then he stood and offered his hand. "Thank you for the information. I appreciate it."

He stood there in silence with his hand extended and a simple smile on his face as he waited for Gabby to respond. I wasn't sure who to bet on, but I was thrilled when Gabby finally gave in, stood, and took Jake's hand in hers. "I must say, you're a little more formidable than I thought you'd be," Gabby conceded with a frown.

Jake just laughed, and to my surprise, Gabby joined in before she walked away.

After she was gone, I asked Jake, "What was that all about?"

"What are you talking about?" he asked as he sat back down and continued to study the menu.

"You know exactly what I'm talking about. That last bit at the end when you got her to leave," I said.

"Suzanne, it's going to take more than someone like Gabby Williams to back me down, no matter how formidable this town might think she is. I wanted her to know that I wasn't going to put up with it, and she got the message, loud and clear."

"Why do I feel as though I should be taking notes on how to handle her in the future?" I asked him with a smile.

"No notes necessary. Just watch and learn," he said with a smile, and then Jake signaled to Trish.

She joined us quickly, and when she got to our table, she asked, "What would you two like?"

Jake pointed to me first, and I ordered a burger and

fries. After I was finished, he held up two fingers as he added, "We'll take two."

"Coming right up," Trish said as she hurried away to place our order.

Evidently the way Jake had handled Gabby had not gone unnoticed among the current patrons of the Boxcar Grill. No one else dared approach us after Gabby's abrupt dismissal, something that I was most thankful for.

While we waited for our food, Jake asked me quietly, "Suzanne, what do you think of Gabby's information?"

"Well, I suppose that it's fair to say that we're friends in the oddest sort of way, but I'm by no means the woman's biggest fan."

"That's not what I asked you."

"I wasn't finished answering yet. There's something you should know about her. If Gabby tells you something, you should take it seriously. She has more leads in this town than anyone else, so if she smells smoke, you can bet your badge that there's a fire somewhere nearby. There may only be a kernel of truth within everything that she says, but you can rest assured that it's there if you dig hard enough for it."

"That's good to know. Do you know Robby Chastain personally?"

"Sure," I said. "He used to be an electrician. The day that man retired from his job, he invested every dime of money he had and every ounce of energy into making his yard a showplace. It's no wonder that tree drove him crazy. I know exactly which one Gabby had to have been talking about. It's an old beaten-down oak clearly in its last days. To be honest with you, it looks as though a light breeze would knock it over, but for some reason, Evelyn was attached to it."

Jake shook his head. "I still can't believe that it's motive enough to commit murder."

"You heard Gabby. There's more history to the story than that."

"The question is, how do we uncover the rest of it?" he asked me.

"Excuse me. Did you mean 'we' as in 'you and me' or 'we, the police'?"

He shrugged before he spoke. "Well, I doubt that I can drag the man into the interrogation room and ask him about it," Jake said. "What you said earlier might be valid after all. Suzanne, I know that you and Grace have solved cases in the past, ones that baffled Chief Martin. I'm not discounting your ability to get facts that law enforcement can't."

"Oh, stop," I said with a smile. "You're making my head swell."

"That being said," Jake continued, ignoring my comment, "I don't want you pushing anyone too far. Your job is to provide me with information. I don't want you and Grace taking any chances on your own, do you understand that?"

"We both know that I can't guarantee that," I said, "especially since one of our suspects is going to be a killer."

"I know that, but you don't have to press your luck."

"So then, do we have your permission to dig into this case?" I asked, wanting to make sure that we were clear on it.

"Conditionally, yes," he said a little reluctantly.

"Hey, we'll take what we can get," I said. "Thank you for the faith that you're putting in us."

"Just don't make me regret it, okay?" Jake asked.

"We'll do our best. Wow, is that our food already?" I asked him as I saw Trish approach carrying a large tray.

"I hope so. I'm starving," he said.

It was indeed our meal, and as we ate, we discussed a dozen different things, but none of the topics was murder. It was a nice respite from what we'd been talking about before, and I was glad for it. After we ate, Jake pulled out his wallet as he grabbed the bill.

"So, you're going to talk to Robby Chastain, right?" he asked.

"As soon as I can find Grace," I said. "What are you going to do?"

"I have someone else I need to speak with," he said, avoiding my glance.

"Are you going to go look for Julie Gray? I might be able to help with that. I have connections in Union Square, remember?"

"I'm not about to forget the formidable DeAngelis family at Napoli's," he said. "But no, I won't be going there until later."

"So then, if you're not going there, where exactly are you headed?" I asked him again. Why was he being so reticent about telling me? And then I knew. "You're going to go talk to my mother, aren't you?"

"What makes you ask that?" Jake said, not bothering to come straight out and lie to me.

"Why else would you be so evasive with me? Besides, it's a good move. Momma just sold the building where Evelyn was murdered. She might have some useful information for us."

"For me," Jake tried to correct me.

I had to laugh. "If you think you're going to interrogate my mother without me going with you, you are seriously delusional, my friend."

"Who said anything about an interrogation?" Jake asked. "I'm just going to have a pleasant conversation with her about the circumstances surrounding the sale."

"If it's just a conversation, then there's no reason that I shouldn't go with you," I said. "After all, how official can it be?"

"I'm not going to win this one, am I?" Jake asked after pausing a moment.

"Not a chance."

"Then let's go," he said as he stood.

"Why do I feel as though I won that round a little too

easily?" I asked him after we paid and we were walking
back to the cottage.

"In all honesty, it might just help having you there."

I stopped walking and looked at him. "Jake, you're not
afraid of my mother, are you? She's just a little old
thing."

"Her size isn't what intimidates me," Jake admitted.

"You know, sometimes you are smarter than you look."

"I certainly hope so," Jake said, the relief clear in his
voice.

I knew that my mother could be a mighty combatant,
and I always loved having her in my corner, but Jake was
right to be wary of her. If he took the wrong tone with
Momma, she'd eat him for breakfast, and what was more,
everyone involved knew it.

"Are you going to have any trouble with the chief?" I
asked him.

"No, he understands the situation. He might just be
local law enforcement, but he really is a pro, Suzanne.
You don't give him enough credit sometimes."

"Maybe not," I replied. I'd actually wondered the same
thing myself. I had been the police chief's biggest critic
at times in the past, and now that he was married to my
mother, I realized that it was time I adjusted my attitude
toward the man. I wouldn't go so far as to call him my
stepfather, though technically it was true, but that didn't
mean that he didn't merit a modicum of respect from me,
given his changed status in my mother's life.

I glanced over at Jake and saw his open mouth. "What
is that look for?" I asked.

"You just agreed with me without an argument," Jake
said.

"Well, don't get used to it. It's not like I want to set
any precedents here."

"Don't worry. I won't take it for granted. I might
relish it a little, though. Are you okay with that?"

"As long as you celebrate quietly," I said with a slight

laugh.

"Come on," Jake said as we got back to the cottage. "Let's go see your mother."

"Can we take my Jeep?" I asked him as I looked over the squad car he'd been given.

"I don't see why not," he said, "even though we are on official police business."

"Don't worry. I won't tell anybody if you don't," I said.

Chapter 7

"My, what a pleasant surprise," Momma said as Jake and I walked into her new place. "I wasn't expecting to see either one of you today."

"Sorry about that, Momma," I told her. "I know that we should have called first, but we need to talk."

"Suzanne, I thought you were going to let me handle this," he told me softly.

I smiled at him. "What on earth made you think that?"

"I don't know, maybe the fact that I'm the one who's in charge of this investigation?" Jake asked.

"Is that what this is about?" Momma asked us. "Hold on one second." She turned and called out to the other room, "Phillip, could you come in here and join us, please?"

Chief Martin came out of the den, and he looked a little surprised to see us there. I knew that it had been nearly a month, but I was still wrapping my head around the fact that the police chief and my mother were married and living together as husband and wife. Every time I went over there, I was honestly startled to find him in the house.

The chief nodded at Jake, smiled briefly at me, and then he asked my mother, "What's this about?"

"They are here to discuss Evelyn's death," Momma said.

The chief looked immediately uncomfortable when he heard that bit of news. "Dorothea, you know that I'm not supposed to get involved with this investigation."

"Don't worry. It's clear that you aren't trying to solve the case," Momma said in a dismissive tone of voice. "But Jake and Suzanne are here to talk with me about what happened to your ex-wife, and I think you should be a part of the discussion."

"As the police chief?" I asked her.

"No, as my husband," Momma said.

"I don't have any objections to you being here, Chief," I said, and then I turned to Jake. "Do you?"

"No, it's fine with me," he said, suddenly aware that he'd clearly lost control of the interview before it had even had a chance to begin. "This shouldn't take long."

"Take your time, dear," Momma said as she patted her husband's hand. "We have nothing to hide."

Jake looked steadily at the chief for a few seconds before he spoke again. "Are you sure that you're okay hearing this? I completely understand why it wouldn't be easy for you to be involved in this case in any way, shape, or form."

"I appreciate you asking, but it's fine. Evelyn and I made our peace, what there was of it, years ago. I wasn't the woman's biggest fan, and she certainly wasn't mine, but she *was* my wife for many years. It was a bad way for her to go."

"There was nothing anyone could do about it. Accidents happen, my love," Momma said reassuringly.

It was too big an opening to ignore. "Only it wasn't exactly an accident after all."

"What are you talking about?" the chief asked. "Jake, I know that you had your doubts at the scene, but have you uncovered anything else that makes you certain that it was anything but exactly what it looked like, that Evelyn slipped and fell in a dark building that wasn't safe to be walking around in?"

"I'm afraid that I have," Jake said. "I don't want to get into the specific reasons with you just yet, but suffice it to say that this is now an official murder investigation being conducted by the North Carolina State Police."

It sounded kind of ominous the way that he said it, and I felt the hairs on the back of my neck stand on end as he spoke. Jake was in full police inspector mode, and again, I almost didn't recognize his voice without its normal warmth reserved for me. It would take some getting used to hearing him speak in such an authoritative manner.

"If it was indeed murder, then what can we do to help, Jake?" Momma asked as she gently touched the chief's shoulder. It was clear at that moment that she truly loved him, something that I hadn't doubted, but still couldn't get used to seeing.

"I need to know why she was inside that building in the first place," Jake said. "It just doesn't make sense her being there."

"How odd. It makes perfect sense to me," Momma said.

"Would you care to enlighten me?" Jake asked her.

"I'd be happy to. I had no problem discovering that Evelyn was in that building. After all, she owned half of it. Why shouldn't she be there?"

"What?" the chief asked her incredulously. "Why didn't you tell me that before?"

"I honestly didn't see that it mattered," Momma replied as she turned to him. "Phillip, I own a great many properties in and around April Springs, and do a fair amount of business on a daily basis. Is it your contention that I should tell you about every transaction that takes place just because we're married now?"

"No, of course not. We agreed that your business was just that when I signed the prenup."

"You have a prenuptial agreement?" I asked loudly.

Momma frowned. "Of course we do. I signed one as well."

"Not that I have any real assets to protect," the police chief said good-naturedly. "I was happy to do it. After all, your mother was just looking out for your inheritance on down the road."

"I don't want to talk about this," I said suddenly. Thinking of my mother planning for her own mortality, a reasonable, even responsible, thing to do, was more than I wanted to consider at the moment, especially since death had just paid us all a visit way too close to home.

"Suzanne, we don't have to say another word about it, since it's not the subject of our discussion," Momma said, and then she turned back to her husband. "Honestly, I didn't think you'd want to know about my business deal with Evelyn. What good could it do for you to learn about it? I thought it would cause you only pain, and I was trying to protect you."

"I don't need protection, Dorothea. I'm a grown man," he said. "You should have told me."

Momma frowned again, and after a moment's consideration, she nodded. "You're right, Phillip. I'm sorry. I made a mistake. Please forgive me."

Wow. I had never seen anywhere near that kind of capitulation on her part in our dealings in the past as mother and daughter, and I wanted to scream at the chief to quit while he was ahead, but instead, he replied, "It's okay this time, but don't let it happen again." If he hadn't added a smile at the last second, I would have been in fear for his life, but my mother just grinned at him in return. Who *was* this woman?

"What I really want to know is where she got the money to buy even half of that building," the chief said. "I know she didn't get it from our divorce settlement. I didn't have much to begin with, and all she got was half of that. It wasn't anywhere near the cash she'd have to have had to buy anything on that scale."

"I wasn't supposed to know anything about it," Momma said, "but Beatrice told me in confidence that Evelyn inherited quite a bit from her great aunt, Ruth. From what I gathered, it was in the neighborhood of a half a million dollars, if Beatrice is to be trusted."

"That's the same figure that we heard," I said, and Jake nodded in agreement. It appeared that Gabby's information, at least about Evelyn's inheritance, had been spot on.

"Did Ruth finally kick the bucket?" the chief asked.

"She was an odd bird, but I figured that she'd find a way to live to see a hundred."

"Evidently she didn't quite make it there, though she wasn't that far off," Momma said. "Anyway, Beatrice told me that Evelyn wanted to go into business, but she was afraid to do it on her own. Since Beatrice had run a few shops successfully in the past, Evelyn convinced her that they should be partners. Evelyn provided the lion's share of the financing, and Beatrice would provide the expertise in their daily business operations."

"What kind of business were they going to open?" I asked Momma. "Please tell me it wasn't going to be a donut shop."

"As a matter of fact, it was going to be a candle store," Momma said. "They had a name picked out for it and everything: Wax, Wicks, and Us. I'm afraid that dream is gone forever."

"What happens to the building now?" Jake asked.

Momma thought about it, and then she said, "You'll have to ask Beatrice, but while we were finalizing the sale, I overheard them talking about having just visited their business attorney next to the yarn shop where she shops in Union Square. They arranged for a partnership agreement between them so that if one partner died, the other would inherit the entire business and all of its assets."

"So, that would give Beatrice a motive for murder," Jake said. "What's the building worth?" he asked Momma.

"What did they pay for it, or how much was its value? They aren't exactly the same questions, are they?" she asked with a slight smile.

"Let's just deal with actual value," Jake said.

"I put its value at one hundred and seventy-five thousand dollars," Momma said, "though they paid a tad more than that."

"So it's a substantial amount," Jake said.

"I suppose two hundred thousand dollars could be considered significant in most circles, but is it enough to make someone commit murder?"

"That's what I intend to find out," Jake said. "Do you have any suggestions as to who I should speak with in my investigation?" He turned to the chief and added, "That question is for you as well."

"I don't know many folks around here who really liked Evelyn besides Gabby Williams, but I can't think of a soul who might want to see her dead," the chief said.

"All I can say is that I suggest you speak directly with Beatrice," Momma said.

"I'd planned on doing that soon enough," Jake replied.

"Then I'm afraid that I've told you all that I can."

"Good enough," Jake said as he started to stand. "Thank you both for your time." He offered his hand to the police chief, who took it. Jake added to him, "Sorry to put you through this. I know this wasn't easy for you."

"Just catch whoever did this so I can get my town back," the chief said firmly.

"Hey, you're still in charge of keeping the peace in April Springs. Don't forget that. I'm just working one case."

"Maybe so, but we both know that it doesn't play out that way. It's an all-or-nothing kind of job, and right now, I'm walking a tightrope."

"I'll do what I can," Jake promised him, and then we left.

Once we were outside, I said, "Let's go see what Beatrice has to say for herself."

"What makes you think that you're coming with me?" Jake asked me.

"Hey, I'm your driver, remember? Do you even know where Beatrice lives?"

"No, but I'm sure that I can find out without your help," Jake said.

"Maybe so, but have you considered the possibility that Beatrice might speak a little freer if I'm there as well?"

"Suzanne, I'm not going to deputize you; you know that, don't you?"

"That's a shame, because I'd love to have my own badge, but honestly, I don't want to be anything official. No offense, but you have too many rules that you have to follow for my taste."

"Funny, I kind of like playing by the rules," Jake said.

"Then you're right where you belong," I said. "Come on. Take me with you. What do you have to lose?"

"Suzanne, what if someone complains to my boss that I've got a civilian tagging along on my investigations? It's one thing for you to go with me to see your mother, but it's something entirely different if you accompany me to interview suspects."

"Do you think Beatrice did it?" I asked him.

"I can think of two hundred thousand reasons that she might," he said.

"I personally can't imagine killing anyone for money," I said.

Jake smiled slightly. "That's just one of the reasons that I love you. But that doesn't mean that you can go with me when I do my job."

"Fine," I said. I knew that he was right. There was no way that I was going to win this particular battle. Besides, I had a hunch that Beatrice wouldn't give Jake the whole story, but she might tell Grace and me later, if we asked her in just the right way. "Let's get you back to that squad car so you can go work on your investigation."

Jake didn't move off Momma's porch, though. "Suzanne, what's going on?"

"What do you mean?" I asked him in my most innocent manner.

"You're giving up too easily," he said with a frown. "I don't like it."

"Mister, you need to make up your mind. I can either

cooperate with you, or I can fight you every step of the way, but I cannot do both."

"You're still not dropping this, are you?"

"I am not," I said. "When the police chief said those vows to my mother, no matter how I felt about it, he became family, and I'm not about to see him get into trouble over this."

"No one's saying that he's a suspect," Jake said evenly.

"Does that mean that you've ruled him out?" I asked him.

"I can't do that, either," Jake admitted. "The ex-husband, especially in a case where the divorce is contentious, is always a suspect until he can be ruled out."

"Then there you go."

Jake sighed, and then he said, "I know I can't stop you from nosing around, but stay out of my way, okay? And don't take any chances you shouldn't."

"Who exactly is going to arbitrate that? You?"

"You know what I mean, Suzanne," Jake said.

Momma saved me from answering when she came outside. "What are you both still doing here? I thought you had already left."

"We were just on our way," I told her, and then I looked at Jake. "So, are you coming, or not? I have to drive you to your squad car, remember?"

"I remember, all right," he said.

After we said our good-byes again to Momma, I drove Jake back to the cottage. He opened his door and started to get out, but I didn't follow suit.

"Aren't you going on inside?" he asked me.

"No, I thought I'd go see Grace first. Her car was in her driveway when we went past her house just now."

I wasn't sure how Jake was going to react to that news, but he just laughed. "Just try to stay out of trouble, okay?"

"We always try," I replied, "but it still has a way of

finding us now and then."

"I don't doubt that for a second. Keep in touch, okay?"

"I will," I said, and before he closed the Jeep's door, I said, "Be safe yourself."

"You know it," he replied. I watched as he got into his squad car and pulled away. I was close on his tail as he drove down the road, but not for long.

When I pulled into Grace's driveway, I saw her heading out to her car. Where was she going? And more importantly, could she drop everything and start investigating with me? I sure hoped so, because I hated doing anything without her.

Chapter 8

"Going somewhere?" I asked Grace as I got out of the Jeep.

"As I matter of fact, I was just about to go out looking for you," she replied with a grin. Grace was always trim and fit, whereas I tended to stay on the curvy side of things. The two of us looked nothing alike, but on the inside, we were sisters in spirit. "What's going on?"

"Actually, I thought I'd do a little digging into Evelyn Martin's murder," I said.

"It was murder?" Grace asked.

I'd forgotten that she didn't know that yet. For that matter, most of the town was probably still ignorant of that particular fact. Was there some way we could use that to our advantage? I'd have to think about that possibility before it became common knowledge.

"Well, at least that's what Jake thinks, and until I learn differently, I'm going to stick with that theory," I said.

"Hang on a second. Back up. Why does Jake have an opinion one way or the other about what happened to Evelyn? I figured he'd be on his way back to Raleigh by now."

"That's right, you haven't heard. There was a slight change of plans," I said. "His boss assigned him to this case, since the police chief's ex-wife is the victim."

"Boy, that's what I get for being so conscientious. I go and do my job for one day and the whole world changes. Is Jake at least still staying with you?"

"As far as I know," I said. "We haven't really gotten around to discussing that yet. Why wouldn't he?"

"As far as I'm concerned, that's right where he belongs," she said. "Some tongues in town may wag about it, though."

"Let them flap all they want to. He's a hero, and they should never forget it. A little gossip isn't enough to even worry about."

"Agreed. So, he doesn't mind the fact that we're digging into his case?" Grace asked.

"I don't know if I'd go that far, but he knows that we're going to do it regardless of whether he approves or not. I think he's resigned himself to the fact that we're going to be working on it, too."

"I'll bet that went over like a lead balloon," Grace said.

"Let's just say we need to make sure that we don't irritate him *too* much," I answered. "I'd hate to solve the case but lose Jake in the process."

"You're not going to lose Jake. Anybody who has ever seen him looking at you would know that."

"I guess so, but I'm still not going to take him for granted. So, are you up for it?"

"I'm ready and raring to go," Grace said. "Let me change out of this suit and I'll be your sidekick in crime fighting."

"That sounds good to me," I said as I followed her back inside.

As Grace changed her clothes into something more casual, she asked me, "So, who should we talk to first?"

"Jake and I have already spoken with Momma about the building sale. I should catch you up on where things stand now before we get started." I proceeded to bring Grace up to date, and by the time she was ready to go, I'd told her everything that I'd been able to learn so far. However, I'd left the details Jake had shared with me in confidence intentionally vague and hoped that Grace wouldn't notice.

"Suzanne, what aren't you telling me?" she asked.

So much for my attempt at subterfuge. "Jake made me promise not to be more specific about a few of the details. As a matter of fact, I might have said too much already."

"Okay, I get that," Grace said. "I'm just going to have to rely on you to lead the way on this case."

"Wow, you're taking that news better than I'd even hoped you would," I said.

"A promise is a promise. I totally get it, Suzanne. Can you at least tell me who our suspects are at this point?"

"That I can do. If we discount the chief, so far there's Evelyn's business partner, Beatrice Ashe; her next-door neighbor, Robby Chastain; and her second cousin, Julie Gray."

"That's a pretty big list this early in the game," Grace said.

"Knowing Evelyn, I've got a hunch that the parade is only going to get longer the more we investigate."

Grace nodded. "She did have a way of making enemies the way most puppies make new friends. I'm guessing that we're going to talk to Beatrice first, right?"

"Wrong. Sorry, but that's where Jake is headed. We have to skirt around the edges, so I thought we'd go talk to Robby instead."

"Why exactly would Robby want to kill her?" Grace asked as we got into my Jeep.

"Evidently they've been battling for quite a while over a great many things. Apparently, the current dispute involved an old oak tree that straddled their property line."

"Let me guess. Robby wanted to keep it, and Evelyn wanted to chop it down."

"You're right, except it's just the opposite of that. Robby thought it was an eyesore, but Evelyn loved it anyway."

"Boy, you think you know someone, and then they go and do something like that," Grace said. "I never figured Evelyn to be a friend of nature."

"Hey, what can I say? We're all complicated," I said.

As we drove to Robby's place next door to Evelyn's, Grace asked, "Would he really kill her over a stupid tree?"

"Probably not, but from what I've heard, there was a

great deal more to it than that."

"What exactly might that be?"

I grinned at her as I admitted, "I haven't a clue. That's why we're going to go talk to him."

When we got there, though, all we could hear was the loud whining noise of a chainsaw.

"Boy, he didn't waste any time taking care of that, did he?" I asked Grace as we got out of the Jeep.

"It must have been pretty important to him," she replied.

"Let's go see if we can find out exactly why."

It took us a full minute to get Robby's attention. The tree in question was already down on the ground and was currently being cut up into fireplace-log-sized pieces.

When he finally saw us, Robby shut off his saw and set it aside. After taking off his ear protectors and his safety glasses, the older man wiped the back of his brow with his hand. "Hey, Grace. How are you doing, Suzanne? Wow, I forgot how hard it was to cut down a tree."

"Is this the same tree that you and Evelyn were squabbling over?" I asked him.

Robby shrugged. "We were, but yesterday she gave me her blessing to cut it down." I looked at him skeptically, and he added, "If you don't believe me, you can ask her yourself."

Was he telling the truth? Was Robby ignorant of the fact that his neighbor was dead, or was he playing a part for our benefit? "You haven't heard the news?"

"What news is that?" he asked as he kicked at one of the branches he'd taken off earlier.

"Evelyn's dead, Robby."

It didn't register at first. After a moment, he looked hard at me. "What are you talking about, Suzanne? Have you been sniffing too much frosting in that donut shop of yours?"

"It's true," Grace said.

Robby slumped down on the stump where the tree had just stood. "You've got to be kidding me."

"It's not something that we'd joke about," I said. "I'm guessing that you didn't know."

"No, I hadn't heard a thing about it. Then again, I've been working with my chainsaw all day. I couldn't get it to start, so I practically had to rebuild it before I could get it running again. What happened to her? Was it a car accident?"

"She was murdered," I said calmly, hoping to see some kind of reaction.

He had one, and it was immediate. "Hang on one second. I sure didn't do it, if that's why you're here. I had no more beefs with the woman after we resolved this thing about the tree."

Grace asked him, "Robby, did anyone see you working on your saw today?"

"I highly doubt it. I was in the garage by myself," Robby said. "That doesn't mean that I killed her, though. What happened? You didn't say?"

"Somebody pushed her through a hole in the floor and she died in the basement."

"Over there?" Robby asked as he stared at Evelyn's house. "That's impossible. I would have at least seen the ambulances and heard the police sirens if that were true. I doubt my hearing protectors could have stopped those."

"I didn't say it was in *this* basement," I said.

"It must have been at the candle shop, then," Robby said.

"How did you know about that?" I asked him suspiciously. As far as I knew, Evelyn and Beatrice hadn't been telling anyone about their plans for their future business venture yet. If that was really the case, then how did Robby know about it?

"She told me yesterday when she came over to give me

permission to cut down this tree. She didn't care about it anymore, since she was going to buy a new place to live, anyway."

"She was leaving her home? Do you happen to know why?" Grace asked.

"Well, it certainly wasn't because of me. Evelyn told me that she recently came into some money, and she planned on blowing every dime she hadn't already spent on a new house. To be honest with you, I don't think she ever liked this tree any more than I did. Having me cut it down saved her from having to pay someone else to do it."

"Robby, I've got a question for you, and it's important. Did anyone else hear your conversation with Evelyn yesterday?" I asked him.

He looked hard at me for a few seconds before he answered. "Suzanne, you're asking me an awful lot of questions for a donutmaker. What business is any of this of yours, anyway?"

"You know me. I'm just a concerned resident of April Springs," I said.

"You're more than that, and we both know it. Do you think folks in town haven't been talking about you and Grace sticking your noses into murder investigations where they don't belong?"

"We may have helped out the police every now and then," I admitted. "So what?"

"You've done more than that, and you both know it. Well, you two aren't going to pin this murder on me. I didn't kill her. Evelyn and I finally patched things up between us, but if you don't believe me, then that's just your own bad luck. Now if you'll excuse me, my break's over. I have some firewood to cut while I've still got the energy."

"We're not finished talking to you," Grace said as he slipped his ear protection back on.

Grinning at her, Robby tapped the earmuff and shouted,

"Sorry, but I can't hear a thing that either one of you are saying."

I was about to yell loud enough for him to hear me even over the earmuff protection when he started the chainsaw back up and attacked part of the trunk of the tree again.

I tapped Grace's shoulder, and we headed back to the Jeep.

"But I'm not finished with him," she said once we got far enough away that we could talk in relative peace over the noise.

"Well, it's pretty clear that he's finished with us," I said.

"Suzanne, do you believe his story?"

"I know that it's awfully convenient, but that doesn't necessarily mean that it's a lie," I said as I pulled out my cellphone.

"Who are you calling?"

"I'm telling Jake what Robby just told us."

"Is that how we're going to be handling this case?" Grace asked me. "Are we giving your boyfriend full and complete cooperation along the way?"

"No, we're giving law enforcement information that might help them solve the case," I replied with a smile.

"It's the same thing, isn't it?"

"Grace, I've seen what going against Chief Martin can do. I'm not about to risk alienating Jake."

"I get that," she said as she nodded her acceptance. "It's just going to be odd, that's all."

"Don't worry. I'm sure that we'll get used to it."

Jake answered his phone, and I said, "Grace and I happened to be driving by Evelyn's house when we saw Robby Chastain cutting down the oak tree he and Evelyn had been fighting about."

"How much of a coincidence am I supposed to believe at this point?" Jake asked.

"That's entirely up to you. Would you like to hear

what he had to say?"

Jake sighed, and then he said, "Sure, why not?"

"Robby claimed that he didn't know that Evelyn was dead, let alone murdered. He told us that last night the two of them agreed to get rid of the tree, and that things were all patched up between them."

"Do you believe him?"

"We're not entirely sure one way or the other," I said. "It's just all a little too convenient for us to swallow, if you know what I mean."

"No one else heard this alleged conversation, did they?" he asked.

"No, and it gets worse. Robby claims that he's been in the garage all day working on his chainsaw. Nobody saw him or talked to him the entire time."

"So, he doesn't have an alibi," Jake said.

"That's true, but if you can find someone who saw him today someplace *other* than his garage or his side yard, then you know that he lied to us about it. That's something, anyway."

"I have to give you credit. It's more than I've gotten so far."

"Wasn't Beatrice cooperative?" I asked him.

"I couldn't find her," Jake admitted. "She wasn't at work or at her house. I'm going to give up on her for now and go find Julie Gray."

"Good luck with that," I said. I decided to hang up before Jake asked me what Grace and I would be doing next. I didn't want to admit what I had in mind, and I hoped that he didn't call back to ask me.

"How did that go?" Grace asked.

"Surprisingly well, as a matter of fact."

"You didn't stay on the phone long."

"That's because I didn't want him to ask me what we were going to do next," I said.

"Would you care to share our plans with me? I'm curious about what comes next myself."

"Jake looked for Beatrice at home and at work, but she wasn't at either place. He's giving up for the moment, but I don't think that we should."

"What did you have in mind?" Grace asked me.

"Well, when Momma was talking, she mentioned something that I think Jake might have missed."

"What's that?"

"She told us that Beatrice shopped at a yarn shop in Union Square near her attorney's office. I wonder if there's any chance that she's there right now?"

"Shouldn't you give Jake a heads-up about that?" she asked me.

"I'm as willing to cooperate with the police as the next gal, but he heard it just as clearly as I did. As far as I'm concerned, that yarn shop is fair game."

"Then let's go to Union Square," Grace said.

Chapter 9

"Should we pop into Napoli's and say hello while we're so close?" Grace asked as we pulled into a parking space in front of the Yarn Barn. The business was right across the street from my favorite Italian restaurant, a charming little establishment owned by Angelica DeAngelis and her lovely daughters.

"We'd better stick to the business at hand," I said. "After all, Beatrice might not even be inside."

"If she's not, we could always ask Angelica if she has any ideas."

"Grace, did you skip lunch again?" My best friend was notorious for working through her noon meal in order to finish her work early. As for me, I wouldn't consciously skip a meal on a bet.

"I could eat," she acknowledged.

"Then we'll take care of your tummy later, but first we have to find Beatrice. I hope she's in there."

"So do I," Grace said. "After we find her, then I can satisfy my appetite."

Unfortunately, the yarn shop was devoid of customers.

A lone employee was restocking brightly colored yarn skeins, but she stopped when we walked in. "May I help you?"

"No, thanks," Grace said as she started to leave.

"Hang on a second," I told her, and then I turned back to the clerk. "Has Beatrice Ashe been here today by any chance?"

"You missed her by half an hour," the woman said. "Are you friends of hers?"

"Yes," I said at the exact time that Grace answered, "No."

"Well, you need to make up your minds," the clerk said good-naturedly.

"I am, but she hasn't met Beatrice yet," I said. "That's why we came in here. We were hoping to remedy that."

"Then try Napoli's," the woman said. "I'll bet she's still there."

"Thank you," I said as Grace and I hurried out.

"See? My instincts were right," my best friend said with a grin. "I told you that we should have gone to Napoli's first."

"Admit it. You just got lucky," I said happily as we headed for the restaurant.

"You know how I feel about luck," she replied. "Sometimes it's better to be lucky than good."

"I'd rather be both if I get the choice."

"Who wouldn't?" Grace asked as an older woman with a bag from the yarn shop exited the restaurant. "Is that her?"

"It is," I said as we approached her. "Hi, Beatrice. Do you have a second?"

"You look familiar, but I'm not sure where I know you from," she said suspiciously as she held her purse tightly against her body.

We'd met a few times, but evidently I hadn't made all that big an impression on her. "I'm Dorothea Hart's daughter, Suzanne, and this is my friend, Grace Gauge."

That loosened Beatrice up. "Your mother drives a hard bargain, but I like her."

"I do, too, but I know exactly what you mean."

"How could you possibly know that?" she asked me.

"Try getting her to agree to let you go to a school dance with Mitchell Bloom when you're sixteen years old," I said with a grin. "By the time we got out of there, she made Mitchell promise everything but to carry me home piggyback. He was so intimidated by her that I was home a good hour before my curfew."

"I don't have any trouble believing that. The question begs itself to be asked, were you two looking for me, or was this meeting just a coincidence?"

"Truthfully, we'd love to talk with you if you have a second," I said.

The older woman glanced at her watch. "I suppose it couldn't hurt, but be warned, I don't have much more than that. I can give you two minutes, but that's about it. I'm heading home to meet someone."

"Is it about selling the building you just bought with Evelyn Martin?" Grace asked her.

"What are you talking about? That's not mine to sell," she said huffily.

"At least not yet," Grace amended. "We understand that you had a survivorship clause in your partnership agreement, though."

"I need to fire that lawyer and report him to the bar for talking out of turn," she said.

"That's not where we heard it."

"Of course it wasn't," Beatrice said as she shook her head. "You got that straight from your mother, didn't you?"

"Is it true, then?" I asked her.

Beatrice shrugged. "I suppose it can't hurt anything admitting it. Yes, Evelyn insisted that we agree to share the business fifty-fifty. I couldn't match her financial investment, not even close, actually, but I was bringing my expertise to the table. Now I'm afraid that particular dream is ruined forever."

"Does that mean that you're not going to open the candle shop without her?" I asked.

"Sadly, I don't have the capital I'd need for supplies, shelving, utilities, licenses, and a dozen other things."

"Then what are you going to do with the building, now that it's yours?"

"I haven't a clue," she said. "Is that why you came all the way to Union Square? Just to pepper me with questions about my relationship with my late business partner?"

"It's one of the reasons we're here," Grace said. "Do

you mind if we ask you where you were this morning?"
"Are you asking me for an alibi?" Beatrice asked her
incredulously.
"Why not? If you have one, it will clear you as a
suspect quickly enough."
Beatrice just shook her head. "What nerve you have. I
didn't kill Evelyn. Why would I? I can't run the
business without her, and I gave up everything to do this
with her. If you're looking for suspects, you should dig
into her love life."
"I didn't even realize that Evelyn was seeing anyone," I
said. "It seemed to me that she wasn't over her ex-
husband yet."
"Well, appearances can be deceiving," Beatrice said a
little smugly. "Perhaps you two don't know everything.
While it's true that Evelyn wouldn't go out with anyone
from April Springs, that didn't keep her from dating
someone here."
"She was going out with someone who lives in Union
Square?" I asked her.
"Yes, a car salesman named Conrad Swoop. They'd
been dating four months, but from what I heard from
Evelyn, they were on the outs lately."
"Do you know why?"
"Apparently, there's a woman named Violet Frasier in
town who thought she and Conrad were exclusive as
well. When she found out about Evelyn, she went
ballistic. It seems Violet doesn't like to share. There are
two wonderful suspects for you right there."
"I can understand why Violet wouldn't care for Evelyn,
but why would Conrad kill her?" Grace asked.
"Evelyn confided in me that she'd foolishly loaned him
some money when she inherited a bundle from her aunt,
and Conrad had no intention of paying her back. It put a
strain on their relationship, and what do you know? Now
that she's gone, he's off the hook for good."
"Not exactly. He still has to pay back the estate," I

said.

Beatrice smiled softly. "Perhaps you'd be right if there were any written record of the transaction. However, I have it on good authority that there isn't any proof that the loan ever took place."

"How do you know so much about Evelyn's personal life?" I asked her.

"Did you forget? We were partners, and besides, Evelyn loved to talk. Sometimes it drove me crazy, but I listened, anyway."

"Is something wrong?" a stunningly attractive woman I was most familiar with asked after opening the door to Napoli's. "Suzanne, Grace, what are you two doing here?"

"Hi, Angelica," I said. "We'll be inside in a minute."

Angelica DeAngelis took the hint and merely nodded as she ducked back inside the restaurant.

"As much as I'd love to stay and chat, I really must go," Beatrice said as she started to walk away.

"We'd be glad to follow you home, if you'd like," Grace said.

"Why on earth would I want you to do that?" she asked with a laugh as she hurried across the street to her car.

After Beatrice was gone, I said, "Did you notice that?"

"Notice what?"

"She neatly ducked our question about having an alibi."

"Maybe that's because she doesn't have one yet," Grace said with a grin.

"You might be right. She was certainly eager enough to give us two alternate suspects, wasn't she?"

"It would be a good way to distract us from looking too hard at her," Grace answered.

"Well, that's not going to happen," I said as I took out my phone.

After he picked up, I asked, "Jake, are you still in Union Square?"

"I'm just getting ready to leave. Why, would you like

me to pick up some takeout for you from Napoli's?"

"Grace and I are just getting ready to go in, as a matter of fact," I said.

"Would you mind if I join you?"

"Are you really hungry enough to eat again? The two of us had a meal not that long ago," I protested.

"And yet you're going into a restaurant right now."

"I'm just going to keep Grace company," I said.

"So, are you telling me that you're not going to order anything for yourself?"

"I might, just to be social," I admitted.

"Then that's what I'll do, too."

"Fine," I said. "I just thought you might like to talk to Beatrice Ashe first."

The playfulness went out of his voice instantly. "Do you know where she is?"

"As of this moment, she's heading home to meet someone," I said. "If you hurry, you might get to her before someone else does."

Jake paused, and then he said, "I suppose you and Grace already spoke with her."

"We tried, but she refused to give us her alibi," I said.

"Suzanne, she's under no obligation to tell you anything."

"That's why we thought you might like a crack at her," I said.

"Okay. I appreciate the tip, but we need to talk about things this evening."

"I can do that," I said, "but for now, Grace and I are going into the restaurant. Would you like anything?"

"No thanks."

He hung up before I could say good-bye.

I stared at my phone for a few seconds before I put it back into my jeans pocket.

"What's wrong?" Grace asked.

"That didn't go nearly as well as I'd hoped it would," I admitted.

"What did you honestly expect, Suzanne? We're stomping around in the middle of his investigation. I didn't figure he'd thank us for it."

"I don't know why not. After all, we told him where he could find Beatrice."

"Sure we did, but only after we chatted with her first. Give him a break. This can't be easy for him to have us looking over his shoulder all of the time, especially when we beat him to one of his suspects."

"I suppose you're right. He wants to talk about it tonight."

Grace grimaced a little. "Ouch. That can't be good."

"Probably not, but I'm not going to worry about it now. Let's go get you something to eat."

"Are you sure that we have time?" Grace asked.

"Jake is going to have his hands full for the next hour unless I miss my guess. Besides, I'm not in any hurry to get the scolding that's probably coming my way. After all, even condemned prisoners get a last meal."

"I'm sure it will all be fine," Grace said as she held the door to the restaurant open for me.

"I hope you're right," I said as I walked inside.

Grace had a full meal, and even though I'd promised myself to eat lightly, I ended up consuming way too many calories before we got out of there. I couldn't hurt Angelica's feelings, could I?

We were both stuffed as we drove back to April Springs.

"I don't envy you this evening," Grace said. "It's not going to be all that pleasant dealing with Jake, is it?"

"I don't know about that. He's usually a very reasonable man," I said a little uncertainly. "I'm sure we'll find a way to work things out."

"I hope so, for both your sakes. Suzanne, you've never been happier. Don't let this case jeopardize that, do you hear me?"

"Yes, Momma," I said with a smile.

She grinned back. "You don't actually expect me to be offended by that, do you? Calling me your mother is the highest compliment you could ever pay me. Besides, we both know that my advice is the exact same thing that your mother would give you if she had the chance."

"Well, she's not going to get the opportunity," I said. "I'm going to deal with the situation with Jake on my own."

"I suppose I could hang around to lend you a little moral support if I had to," she conceded.

"Thanks, but like I said, I can tackle this all by myself," I said.

Halfway back to April Springs, Grace asked, "Are you at all nervous about tomorrow?"

"What about it?" I asked absently. It was growing dark, and a set of headlights on high beams was in my rearview mirror. I tried flipping the mirror to the dimming position, but the inside of the car was still lit up. "What is this guy's problem?" I tapped my brakes, and he backed off. After tapping them twice more, he must have realized that his high beams were on, and they shifted back to their normal intensity. "There, that's better. Now, what were you saying?"

"I was wondering how you felt about going back to the donut shop in the morning," she said. "It's been a month since you've worked there."

"That may be true, but I've popped in every now and then since I left it in Sharon and Emma's hands," I said.

"I know that, but it's going to be a whole different thing running it again. The hours are going to kill you, for one thing."

I didn't tell her that I'd never truly adapted to the new sleep schedule since I'd been taking care of Jake. I seemed to wake up every morning at exactly the same time, regardless of whether I was using an alarm clock or not. "I'll manage."

"Don't forget, you'll be on your feet a lot more, too."

I looked over at her for a second. "Grace, are you saying that I shouldn't go back to Donut Hearts tomorrow?"

"What? Of course not. Everyone knows that's where you belong. I'm just saying that you shouldn't be surprised if it's difficult at first getting used to being back in the saddle."

"Thanks for worrying about me, but I'm sure that I'll manage just fine."

"Of course you will," Grace said. "What do you think Jake's going to say tonight?"

"I'm not sure, but I'm betting that I'll find out soon enough," I said.

We were back in town before long, and I pulled into Grace's driveway so I could let her out and then make my way back to the cottage.

"Good luck," she said as she squeezed my hand before she got out of the Jeep. "Call me later if you need to talk."

"Grace, stop worrying about me. Everything is going to be just fine."

"Just keep repeating that, and maybe it will turn out to be true," she said with a hopeful grin.

I watched her go to her door, unlock it, and step inside before I made my way to the cottage. I wasn't exactly concerned about my impending discussion with Jake, but that didn't mean that I wouldn't appreciate a little time to prepare myself for it.

Unfortunately, that didn't happen.

The police cruiser was already parked in the driveway, and as my headlights swept across the porch as I pulled up, I saw Jake waiting for me there.

It appeared that things were going to get started sooner rather than later, whether I was ready for it or not.

Chapter 10

"Hey, there," I said as I approached Jake. "Can I make you something to eat?"

"I appreciate the offer, but I picked up a sandwich on the way back," he said.

"Sorry about that. It's not quite the golden cuisine I had, is it?" I asked. "Would you like to chat inside? It's getting a little nippy out here."

"If you don't mind, let's do this out here. I'd kind of like to separate this conversation from the rest of our evening, if that's okay with you."

"That doesn't sound good," I said as I took a seat beside him. "Go on. Let me have it. Chances are I deserve whatever I'm about to get."

Jake looked down at his hands for a few moments as he prepared himself to speak. Wow, Grace had been right. This really was going to be bad. "Suzanne, I don't even know where to start," he finally said. "This is the oddest way that I've ever worked a case in my entire career."

"I know that it's not conventional for you," I said, "but when you think about it, we make the perfect team. You shouldn't be upset about it; you should be embracing it."

"Go on. Enlighten me," he said softly.

"Jake, one of the main reasons that you were assigned to this case is because you know so many of the people involved, right?"

"Certainly that's part of it," he said grudgingly.

"Well, when you think about it, that's where Grace and I can help you. You look at things like a cop. You can't help it. It's been ingrained in you from your first day at the academy."

"That's a good thing, Suzanne. Need I remind you that I'm very good at what I do?"

"You don't have to convince me," I said. "I'm your

biggest fan."

"Then why won't you let me solve this case by myself?" He was clearly frustrated with the situation, and it hurt me to realize that it was my fault.

"I'm good at what I do, too," I said. "Grace, George and I have solved several murders in the past. Even Chief Martin is willing to admit that we've played vital roles in some of his investigations."

"The chief and I are two very different law enforcement officers, though."

"I'm not trying to take anything away from you. What I want to do is make things easier for you, not harder."

"How are you planning to do that?"

"Think about it. Grace and I are able to ask questions that you aren't. We can go places you're not welcome, and we know where a lot of the skeletons are buried around town. Don't forget, too, that our reach goes beyond April Springs. We have people we can talk to in Union Square as well."

"Don't sell me too short. I've got a hunch that Angelica would talk to me, too," Jake said.

"Of course she would, but will she tell you the same things that she tells me? I don't think so. Jake, the two of us have a history that you can't touch."

"I guess what I hate most about this situation is the idea that you're not safe," Jake finally admitted. "Suzanne, I hope you know that my reluctance to involve you in this case has nothing to do with my ego. Trust me, I'll take help wherever I find it. You've just come too close in the past to being hurt while you've been tracking down killers. If something happened to you while I was investigating, I'd never be able to forgive myself."

I could easily understand how he felt, but I couldn't let that run my life. "I get it. I know firsthand how it felt when you were shot, but I'm not going to try to stop you from doing your job."

Jake stood at that point and began to pace around the

porch. "But you're a donutmaker. You're not a trained investigator."

"I know that. Grace and I are both well aware of our limitations. We never take any unnecessary chances when we're digging into murder. There's something else that you need to realize. Think about the killers who still might be out there somewhere if we hadn't taken an active role in investigating their crimes. I'm not sure I could live with myself if someone else got hurt when I might have been able to prevent it. When I first got started doing this, I had no idea how much satisfaction I'd get out of helping capture the bad guys."

"It kind of gets in your blood after a while, doesn't it?" Jake asked with the hint of a grin showing.

"So much so that I don't think I can go back to being just a donutmaker anymore. Digging into these crimes has become a part of me, and of Grace as well. Please don't ask us to give that up now."

"What kind of boyfriend would I be if I did that?" he asked lightly.

"Not a very good one, despite the fact that your intentions might be just to protect me. This isn't something I do because I need to. It's something that I *like* to do."

"Maybe you should go to the academy yourself, then," Jake said, halfway serious.

"No, I don't think so. I could never operate within your framework of rules, reports, and regulations. What I'm good at is talking to people, and finding out their secrets. I don't have any desire to put the cuffs on a bad guy, or read them their rights, but I'm delighted if something I do helps capture them. The real question, though, is that something that you can live with?"

"Do I have any choice? I know your mother didn't. She told me herself that in the beginning, she tried her best to get you to stop."

"Let's leave her out of this, shall we?" I asked him.

"This is between you and me. What do you say? Can Grace and I work on the sidelines and help you find whoever killed Evelyn Martin?"

It seemed to take him forever to answer, but when he did, he spoke with a wry smile. "Sure, why not? I know one thing. I'm going to have to learn to try to stop telling you to be careful with every breath I take. Just assume that every time we chat, that's what I'm saying."

"I can do that," I said with a smile.

"Good enough," he said. "And remember, I can't do anything to give either one of you official status of any kind. This isn't some kind of quid pro quo situation. You both need to tell me everything you uncover, but I'm not in the same position. I'm not about to share everything I know with both of you, so you're going to be flying blind sometimes. There's no other way to say it, Suzanne. To a certain extent, you and Grace are both on your own there."

"We don't expect any special treatment from you," I said, and then I smiled at him. "Well, at least not as far as our investigation is concerned."

"Then we should be fine."

"I have one question. Can we still call you if we get in a jam?" I asked.

"I'd better be the first call that you make," Jake said. "But do me a favor. Try not to get into any jams in the first place, okay?"

"Will do, Chief."

"Inspector will do just fine," he said. "Now, I know that we've both eaten, but how about some dessert?"

"I ate more than I thought I would at Napoli's, but I might have a bite of pie before I go to bed."

Jake looked at his watch. "Already? Oh, that's right. In all of the excitement, I forgot that tomorrow was your first day back at Donut Hearts. How excited are you?"

"More than I can express," I said. After another moment's thought, I added, "You know, I could probably get Emma and her mother to keep working at the shop for another week if you'd like me to help you investigate Evelyn's murder."

"Young lady, you need to get back to that donut shop as soon as you can," he said. "Your crime-solving can still be fitted in on your off-hours. Besides, I'm sure that everyone involved wants things back to normal as quickly as possible, including you, deep down."

"You're right, but Grace and I are still planning to be active in the investigation."

"As you've made abundantly clear this evening," he said. "Come on. Let's get that pie."

"You don't have to ask me twice."

As Jake and I enjoyed thin slices of one of the pies Momma had brought by the day before, I wondered how things would be tomorrow. I'd be back at work, and so would Jake. Though he wouldn't be working his post with the state police, that didn't mean that he wouldn't be on the job. Would it change things between us, this new dynamic? I'd been used to taking care of him for the past month, but he was way past needing anything from me now, at least for healing purposes. I hoped that he'd always need me emotionally. I just prayed that wouldn't change once he was running the investigation into Evelyn Martin's murder. I'd seen the professional Jake enough to know how he could get while he was on a case.

It would just be my duty to remind him that the job was one thing, and our relationship was something else altogether.

I had to hit the alarm clock twice before I finally came fully awake the next morning. How did I ever manage all those years on such little sleep? As I took a quick shower, I realized that there would be a nap in my future, and I wondered if I'd have enough energy to investigate anything once I was back on my old schedule. At least I'd have the shop to myself before Emma came in.

I was wrong about that too, though.

When I pulled up in front of Donut Hearts, the lights inside were already on, and Emma's car was parked off to one side.

It appeared that my assistant had beaten me into work on her first day back. I wasn't sure that was a good sign or not as I unlocked the front door and let myself in.

"Hey, Emma. What are you doing here so early?" I asked as I took off my jacket and hung it up in the back room. At least I started to, until I found the hook already occupied by Emma's coat.

"Sorry about that," she said as she reached for her jacket in order to move it.

"Nonsense. You can keep your coat there if you'd like."

"No, it's just a bad habit I got into," she said as she moved the coat to her old spot, a hook closer to the back door. "There, that's better."

"I really don't mind," I said as I put my jacket where it belonged, but it wasn't entirely true. Was I actually upset that Emma had taken my coat hook when she'd been running the donut shop at my request? Wow, I might have had more issues with the situation than I realized.

Emma smiled tentatively after I put my apron on. She said, "I'm sorry I'm early, but I've been used to coming in at this time of the morning for a month, and nobody told my body that I could sleep in a little today."

"That's fine," I said. "I understand completely. I've had a tough time sleeping in myself." I clapped my hands together, and then I said with a smile, "Let's get started, unless you've already made a batch of donuts yourself this morning."

"I'd be lying if I said that I wasn't tempted, but I'm fine going back to the way we had things before."

That's what she told me, anyway, but I wasn't sure that I believed her. I knew that it would have been tough for me to take orders from anyone else once I'd been in charge. I'd have to be careful around Emma until we could figure out how to make things work again without tiptoeing around each other.

I opened the first cabinet and found myself facing row upon row of spices instead of the baking powder I'd been expecting. "What happened here?"

"Mom and I thought it made more sense," she said, "but we can change things back to the way they were. I just figured you might like to see our arrangement before we made any changes."

It was unsettling to find things moved from where I'd been expecting them, but I took a deep breath and said, "Since you're here early, why don't you explain your new system to me and we'll see?"

"That would be great," Emma said. She was so enthusiastic about the new placement of items I used every day that it was all I could do not to show the disapproval I felt. My immediate reaction was to put everything back the way that it had been when I'd left, but I took a deep breath and decided to give her the benefit of the doubt. After she was finished, I leaned back against the counter.

"You hate it, don't you?" Emma asked. "I told Mom that we should put things back the way they were, but she insisted I at least show this to you."

"I'm glad that you did," I said. "There are a few things that I'm going to keep, but I hope you don't mind if I put a few others back where I like them. It's not that they aren't good where they are. They just aren't where I'll be expecting them to be."

"That's fine," she said. "What exactly do you like?"

"Well, I think the new spice arrangement could work," I said.

"What about the flour and sugar storage?" she asked.

I shrugged. "I suppose I could probably get used to that as well."

Emma stared at me for a few seconds without saying a

word, and I was afraid that she was about to cry when she surprised me by laughing loudly.

"What's so funny?" I asked her.

"I just did all of this to mess with you, Suzanne. We kept things the way you had them, but when I got here early this morning, I decided to have a little fun."

I had to laugh as well. "You nearly killed me just now; you know that, don't you?"

As Emma and I started putting things back in their rightful places, she said, "I thought you were going to bite your lower lip in half. Don't worry. I can have this finished in five minutes, and I haven't punched in yet, so it's on my dime."

"I think the joke is at least worth being on the clock for," I said. "Mark your time down, and let's get things back to where they belong."

"It's good to have you back," Emma said with a smile as she noted the time down.

"Are you sure that you're not going to hate going back to being my assistant?"

"I'm positive," she said. "I did have a few ideas I wanted to run past you, though. I'm not trying to upset the system we have working now, but Mom and I came up with a few things that might make both of our lives easier."

"I'm all for that," I said. "Let's hear what you've got."

By the time we had things right again, I'd listened to Emma's pitches. They were all sound, little tweaks in our routine that would indeed make both of our lives better. "Done and done," I said. "I only have one condition before I accept your new ideas."

"What's that?" she asked, clearly concerned about what my request might be.

"I want you to come in early two days a week and make the cake donuts on your own. That will keep your hand in things, and it will have the bonus of allowing me to sleep in a little later two days a week. You'll make more money, and have more responsibility as well. How does that sound to you?"

"It's perfect," she said. "Are you sure you don't mind giving up some control?"

"I turned the whole place over to you for a month," I said. "I think I can at least do that much. I had another thought."

"I'm listening," Emma said.

"When things settle down, I'd love it if you and your mother would be willing to take the shop over for a few weeks again."

"Are you kidding? Mom would love the opportunity to squirrel away more travel funds, and you know me, I'm always saving up, too. What did you have in mind?"

"Jake promised me a trip to Paris, and I plan to take him up on it," I said.

"Good for you," Emma said as she hugged me. "So, I'm willing to wager that familiarity hasn't bred any contempt yet."

"What do you mean?"

"Well, he's been staying with you for a month now. I'm guessing that he's not moving out anytime soon."

"Guess again," I said as I started getting ingredients out to make my cake donut batter. "As soon as he solves this case, he's going back to Raleigh."

"I'm so sorry," Emma said.

"Don't be. I'm all for it," I said as I set up the bowls for different donut mixes.

"Aren't you afraid that you'll be lonely in that cottage all by yourself now that your mom's moved out?" she asked me.

"My mother is a newlywed; I'd hope that she'd live with her groom, and everyone knows that the police chief and me living under the same roof just wasn't going to work. Besides, I'm kind of looking forward to being alone. It's past time, if you ask me. Now, is there anything else ground-shattering that you need to tell me about before we get back into our old routines?"

"No, that's it," Emma said, and then, almost as an afterthought, she added, "Oh, I've been dating someone new for the past few weeks, but it's too soon to say if he's going to be a keeper or not."

"Give it time," I said as I got down my recipe book. "I know that it seems like forever at your age, but there's no rush."

"That's exactly what my mother keeps saying, but I still think this one's here to stay."

"Good for you," I said as I leafed through the copied pages of my book full of recipes. I was a little rusty, but there was no real surprise there. Before my break, I could have done most things blindfolded, but in the interim, I'd lost the knack. No worries; I was sure that I'd be able to get it back soon enough. At the moment, it just felt right being back where I belonged, in the Donut Hearts kitchen well before dawn making treats for all of April Springs to enjoy. Jake had been right.

It was good to be back.

If he felt a tenth as good as I did being back at my old job, he had to be relishing the opportunity to go after a killer again. Truthfully, I'd missed that myself on occasion, though my crime-fighting was strictly on a local level next to his statewide beat. There were months when nothing more exciting than donut sales came into my life, and I was usually pretty grateful for those times, but then again, I didn't shy away from investigating murder when it came into my life.

All in all, it wasn't a bad way to live, if you discounted the killers that popped up every now and then.

Chapter 11

"Hey, what are you doing here so bright and early this morning?" I asked our mayor, George Morris, as I unlocked the door to Donut Hearts when we were first open for business.

"I'm here to celebrate your first day back," he said as he gave me a small bouquet of flowers.

"Thanks," I said as I took them from him. "And tell Polly I said thanks, too."

"What makes you think she had anything to do with this?" George asked me.

"I know you too well, George," I said as I kissed his cheek. Polly was more than the mayor's secretary and assistant. She was also his girlfriend. "If Polly didn't prod your memory that I was coming back, I'll give you six dozen donuts, on the house."

George shrugged. "I couldn't eat that many donuts, anyway. How does it feel being back behind the counter again?"

"Kind of odd so far," I said.

"It must be even stranger having Jake work a case in April Springs," he answered.

"I suppose I shouldn't be surprised that you know about that already."

"As mayor, I'm in the loop about anything happening with our police department," he said, "but I didn't need to wait for official notification to find out what was going on. Jake called me as soon as he talked to his boss yesterday."

"And you're good with the arrangement?" I asked him. Usually folks in charge didn't like having any outside interference when it came to running our town.

"Jake and I are on the same side. If he hadn't done it, I was going to volunteer myself. It just wouldn't look right having Phillip investigating the case himself."

"Funny, I figured you had enough on your hands running April Springs without taking over a criminal investigation, even if you did used to be a cop on the force."

George sighed before he spoke. "To be honest with you, Polly pretty much runs things around here. She just needs me to sign my name now and then, but it wouldn't surprise me if she could sign it better than I can by now."

"You're being overly modest," I said. I knew for a fact that George had his hand in on a dozen decisions every week that impacted all of us who lived in April Springs.

"Not as much as you might think." He stared at the full donut cases, and then said, "I might not have remembered that you were going to be here today on my own, but I did stop and buy the flowers along the way. That's got to at least count for something."

"How about two plain cake donuts and a cup of coffee, my treat?" I offered. That was his regular order anyway, so I wasn't exactly going out on a limb suggesting it.

He nodded. "That's all I'm talking about. They can't be on the house, though."

"Why not?"

"I don't want it to look as though I'm accepting any bribes," George said.

I had to laugh at that. "George, we've been friends forever. If you could do something for me, I wouldn't insult your dignity by bribing you."

"Thank you for that," he said.

As I slid the donuts across to him, I said with a smile, "I wouldn't have to bribe you, would I? I'd just come right out and ask you."

"There you go," he replied with a grin of his own as he paid for his breakfast. "So, what's new with the investigation?"

I turned around as though I were looking for someone else. "Are you talking to me?"

"Of course I am."

"I'm not the one investigating Evelyn's murder," I said levelly.

"Maybe not officially, but I hear that you and Grace have already been knocking on doors asking some tough questions around town."

"Wow, news travels fast around here, doesn't it?" I asked him.

"You know it better than I do. How's Jake feel about you digging into his investigation?"

"He's absolutely thrilled about it," I said with a wry smile.

George took a sip of coffee, and then he said, "Yeah, right. Is he very upset about it? I can talk to him, if you think it might help."

"Thanks for the offer, but we had a long discussion about it last night. We're good."

"For now," George said. "Tread carefully, Suzanne. There's more than a man's pride at stake here."

"Nobody knows that better than I do," I said. "How are your donuts?"

"They are delicious. It's good to see that you didn't lose your touch during your sabbatical."

"Don't give me too much credit. That's one of the most basic donuts I make here."

"You know what I always say. You can't beat a classic," the mayor said with a smile as he finished up his second donut.

"Would you like another one for the road?" I asked George as I got him a paper cup for his coffee to go.

"I'd better not," he said.

"Come on. Live dangerously. I won't tell Polly if you won't," I said.

He just shook his head. "Truth be told, I probably should have stopped at one. Trust me, she'll know the second I walk into the office later. I don't know how she does it, but she knows."

"It's no great secret, George. She gets you, front to back."

"That's what I'm afraid of," he said as he stood. "Welcome back."

"Glad to be here," I said.

Ninety seconds later, I got my second surprise that morning when Jake walked in.

"I didn't realize you were going to be up this early," I said.

"You know how I get when I'm working on a case," he said, and then he gestured to the flowers. "Are those from an admirer?"

"This is embarrassing," I said with a shrug. "Evidently I just can't help that I'm so irresistible. We had so many arrangements in back that we can't even move around in the kitchen. This has become our overflow area."

He laughed as he glanced at the card. "I'm guessing that Polly had a hand in this."

"I didn't realize you were that in sync with the folks around here," I said as I got him one glazed donut and a cup of coffee to go.

"That's why I got this assignment in the first place, remember? So, what are your plans today?"

"I'm going to sell donuts for most of the rest of the morning, and then I'm going to clean up, make the bank deposit, and then maybe take a quick nap."

He raised one eyebrow. "So, you aren't going to do any investigating?"

"Oh, that, too. I forgot. Grace and I are headed out later to chat with a few of our suspects."

He laughed, which was the exact reaction that I'd been hoping for. "Just stay out of trouble," he said as he shook the bagged donut at me. I thought for a second that he hadn't paid, which would have been fine with me, but then I looked down at the counter and saw a five there. That was the best tip that I'd gotten in some time, but it wasn't going to stand. I made change in the register, put a suitable amount in our tip jar, and then I tucked the rest into my front pocket. I'd return it that evening, along with a lecture about how he should learn not to overtip, especially at Donut Hearts.

It was nearing eleven, our standard closing time, and I couldn't wait to lock the doors after I shooed everyone out of the building. Running the place had been tougher than I'd remembered, and I was thrilled about the idea that I wasn't that far from a nap in my near future.

At least I thought so, until I heard a strange woman asking me if I was Suzanne Hart.

"I'm Suzanne," I said. "How may I help you?"

"You don't know me, but I'm Evelyn Martin's cousin, Julie Gray."

She was a mousy little blonde in her late twenties, with sharp eyes and a pinched nose. Her clothes were second-rate, but she had a brand-new manicure, and I could swear the ring on her finger had belonged to Evelyn not that long ago. She didn't need that for identification, though. I could see the resemblance between the two women immediately. "Hi, it's nice to meet you, even under such trying circumstances. I'm so sorry for your loss." It was as automatic as wishing someone a nice day, or saying 'Bless you' when they sneezed.

"Thanks. Suzanne, I was wondering if you could do me a huge favor."

"I'd be glad to do what I can," I said as I rubbed my hands on my apron. "But I'm afraid that I don't have much pull around here, though. You might be better off asking someone else for help."

"From what I've heard, you're exactly the right person I need to speak with. It's about your boyfriend."

"What about him?" I asked her guardedly.

"It's just that he won't tell me anything about what

happened to Evelyn, no matter how much I ask him for specific details. I was hoping that you could put in a good word for me."

Her hopes were in vain. "I'm sorry, but I don't interfere with police business."

Julie bit her lower lip for a moment, and then she said, "That's not what I heard from Evelyn."

I should have closed early when I had the chance. This was my reward for being so dedicated on my first day off. "I'm not sure what your cousin might have told you, but the woman wasn't my biggest fan, not by a long shot, so you should take anything you heard with a grain of salt."

Julie waved a hand in the air. "You don't have to explain my cousin to me. I know better than anyone how capricious Evelyn's affections could be. She's given up on me a dozen times in my life, but she always came back. Like they say, you can pick your friends, but you're stuck with your family for your entire life."

"I happen to love my family," I said, probably acting a little stiffer than I should have. This woman not only looked a little like her cousin, but she had Evelyn's bite as well. Maybe it was a mean gene that passed around the family from generation to generation. If that were so, I was glad that my family tree was planted in a different orchard.

"I'm sure you do, but I'm equally as certain that Evelyn wasn't quite so loveable. Be that as it may, I still want to find out what happened to her."

"And Jake wouldn't tell you anything?" I asked. Surely he had a reason if he were behaving that way toward her. Was she more of a suspect in the murder than I'd realized?

Julie waved a hand in the air. "Oh, he told me about his theory that she had been pushed, and that finding her the way he did made him suspicious that something darker was the cause of it."

I looked at her oddly. "That's all anyone knows at this point. What makes you think that he's holding something else out on you?"

"He wouldn't name a single suspect, for one thing," she said.

"I'm afraid I can't help you there, either."

Julie shrugged slightly, and then she smiled for a moment. "I understand. You might not know anything now, but who knows what the future might hold?" She reached into her purse and pulled out a business card. After scribbling something on it, she handed it to me. "That's got my personal cellphone number on it. I'd be most appreciative if you'd call me the second you learn anything."

I wanted to refuse the card, but the easiest thing for me to do was to just take it from her and then, after she was gone, toss it into the drawer where I kept other pieces of useless information. When I reached for it, she wouldn't let it go, though. Before Julie would release the card, she said in a soft voice, "My cousin has left me a great deal of money, and I promise to reward those who have helped me, if you get my meaning."

"If I can't do it, a bribe is not going to change anything. That kind of motivation is honestly sort of lost on me," I said.

"Don't think of it as a bribe. Consider it motivation and an incentive to help me."

"Call it what you will, but it's not going to change anything."

She looked puzzled by reaction. "But you'll keep the card, right?"

"Sure," I said, "but I make no promises whatsoever. Is that understood?" I realized that there might be a way to leverage her request for information in my favor later on if she continued to be a suspect in her cousin's murder. The most prudent thing to do was go along with her until I had a chance to gather more information about her true relationship with the murder victim. I knew from experience that a great many people claimed warm and loving joy toward some folks after they were gone, but wishing didn't make it true, and the facts were many times quite a bit uglier than anyone let on.

"I get it completely," Julie said, and then she looked around the donut shop as though she just realized what kind of storefront she was currently in. "My, how quaint your place is."

"Thanks. I like it," I said.

"So do I," Emma echoed from the kitchen doorway. How long had she been standing there? "Are we ready to close now, boss?"

I glanced at the clock on the wall and saw that it was three minutes after eleven. I now had the perfect excuse to get myself out of this situation. "I hate to be this way, but we're closed, so unless you feel like pitching in and mopping the floor for us, it's time to go."

I knew my audience. Julie Gray wouldn't voluntarily mop up a floor under any circumstances, even if she thought it might mean securing my help.

"I'd love to, I truly would, but I've got pressing matters dealing with Evelyn's estate. So sorry that I couldn't help."

"I understand completely," I said with my cheesiest smile that meant nothing to anyone who truly knew me. "Good-bye."

"Until we meet again," she said as I opened the door for her, and then I made sure that I locked it once she was standing out on the sidewalk.

Emma asked me, "What was that about? Did you really expect that girl to mop the floor? With those fingernails?"

"It seemed like the easiest way to get rid of her," I admitted. "How are things in back?"

"Ready for inspection, ma'am," she said as she clicked her heels together.

"Since when did we start having inspections around here? If you say that it's clean, I believe you." I gestured to the display cases. "If you'll just box the last of the donuts, you can go ahead and take off."

"I don't mind hanging around if you need me," she said.

"I think you've done more than your share lately," I said, and then I felt a twinge of guilt about how small her check had been, given how hard she and her mother had worked. "I really do wish that I'd been able to pay you and your mother more for all of the hard work you did."

"Don't sweat it, Suzanne. Mom is in heaven planning her next trip, all thanks to you," she said.

"And what about you?"

"It's going where everything else I make goes, straight into my college fund. I've been thinking about something I wanted to run past you."

Was she heading back to school sooner rather than later? I'd lost her once, albeit temporarily, and I hated the thought of losing her again. "You're going back in the fall, aren't you?"

"What? No way. But it does kind of relate to that, when and if I do go."

"Go on. I'm listening."

"I kind of enjoyed my time running Donut Hearts when you were gone, not that I didn't miss you, you understand. It was just really cool being my own boss."

"That's one word that I'd use," I said with a smile. "I have a few others, if you'd like to hear them."

"Believe me, I know the pluses and minuses of running your own business. But I still might want to try something myself later on down the line."

"You want to open a donut shop of your own?" I asked her incredulously.

"Are you kidding? I'm not insane," she said loudly.

"Hang on. I didn't mean it that way."

"I hope that's exactly how you meant it," I said.

"Not a donut shop, but something else for sure. Don't worry. It's going to be a long, long time from now."

"I hope so, but I understand the benefits of being your own boss. Do you have any idea what you might be interested in doing?"

"Not a clue," she said with a smile. "And I don't need to know right now. All I have to do is figure out what classes to take to make it happen."

"I've got a feeling the school might be able to help you with that."

She waved a hand in the air. "Sure, I'm going to talk to them, but the reason I'm telling you now is that I want to ask you a question."

"I'll answer it if it's in my power to," I said.

In a meek voice, she asked me, "Be brutally honest with me. Do you think I've got what it takes?"

I hugged her as I said, "You bet I do. I think you'll be terrific at whatever you decide to do."

"Thanks," Emma said, and then she pulled away a little. "Do you really mean that, or are you just saying it because we're friends?"

"We're more than friends, Emma. I've worked with you side by side for years. You have every characteristic it takes to run a successful small business, at least in my mind. I have complete and utter faith in you, for whatever it's worth."

"Suzanne, it's worth everything to me," she said as she rubbed one eye.

"What do your folks think about your plans?" I asked her.

"Mom's on board, but I haven't told Dad yet. I have a feeling that he wants me to take some journalism classes, but that's not happening."

"Not interested in joining the family business?"

"No way, no how." She studied the display cases and then shrugged. "I'd better jump on those donuts right now," she said with a smile.

"If you do that, we won't be able to give them away," I answered her with a laugh. It was an old joke, one that we told with some frequency, but it broke the serious mood of the situation.

After Emma started boxing donuts, I turned to the cash register and ran our reports as the machine did its magic. I just hoped that we were somewhere close to being balanced. I couldn't take a lengthy time period analyzing where I might have gone wrong.

To my delight, it balanced out perfectly, and by the time I had the day's deposit ready, Emma had the place cleaned up.

"Are you ready to call it a day?" I asked her.

"More than I can tell you," she said. "No offense, but I can't wait to get out of here."

"I'm beat, too," I said. "I'm going to go home, take a shower, and then grab a quick nap. How about you?"

"Actually, I've got a date," she said with a grin. Where did she find the energy after the day we'd just had? Then again, she was quite a bit younger than I was. I took a little solace in that.

After I locked the place up, I carried the leftover donuts out to my Jeep so I could drive to the bank and take care of the day's final order of business.

I never made it there, though.

Someone stopped me before I had the chance to follow through with the rest of my plans for that afternoon.

Chapter 12

"Suzanne, we need to talk," my ex-husband, Max, said as I was stowing the donuts in the backseat of my Jeep. "If you're hungry, you can have a box," I said. "It's got nothing to do with food. I need to ask you something about Emily."

My ex had been dating my good friend for some time, even proposing at one point, though the wedding had never materialized. I knew that Max was serious about her, and I had a hunch that the feeling was mutual. "I suppose I have a minute, but just that. I have to get to the bank, and then I have some other errands to run as well." I wasn't about to tell him that the second task on my list was going back to the cottage and taking a nap. I was worn out! How could a month off do that to me?

"That's fine. I just need to ask you about Dusty Baxter."

"Dusty? What about him?" I remembered the tall, handsome young man who used to live in April Springs, but I couldn't figure out why Max was asking about him. And then I remembered that he'd dated Emily Hargraves before he'd moved to New York.

"He's back," Max said.

"In April Springs? What on earth would possess him to come back here? The last I heard, he was a big success working in finance in New York."

"Evidently he's decided that he's tired of the grind and wants to move back here. Guess what else he wants to do?"

"Does it have something to do with Emily?"

Max frowned. "Of course it does. We were at The Boxcar last night on a date when he sauntered in as though he owned the place. You wouldn't believe the fuss people were making over him."

"Including Emily?" I asked him.

"Her most of all. She invited him to join us at our table, and he had the gall to take her up on it. I had to sit there listening to them relive their glory days. It was all I could do to keep my dinner down."

"You could have always excused yourself and left," I said, being a little meaner than I should have been. Max and I had made our peace quite some time ago, but that still didn't keep me from occasionally taking a few shots at him.

"Wouldn't he have loved that," my ex said. "No, I sat there and smiled, nodded every now and then, and generally pretended to be having the time of my life."

"I'm sure they bought it," I said. "After all, you're an excellent actor."

"Thank you for that," he said. "But it's beside the point. What am I going to do?"

"About Emily? Nothing at all."

"That's it?" he asked me incredulously. "That's the best advice that you've got?"

"Listen, Max. They broke up for a reason, and I doubt it had anything to do with the fact that he was leaving town. Emily cares for you now." I studied him a moment, and then I added, "It's not like you to be so insecure."

"I know, right? There's something about that guy that just puts my teeth on edge."

I patted his shoulder. "Stop worrying about it, and for goodness sake, don't let Emily sense how you really feel. The best way to drive her back into Dusty's arms is to let Emily see how worried you are about him. Just try to remind her why the two of you are together whenever you get the chance, but don't force anything. She'll be able to smell it from a mile away."

"Thanks. You're right. That's good advice."

"Whoever dreamed I'd be giving you dating tips when we first divorced?" I asked.

"Certainly not me, but it's not going to go unappreciated." Max paused a moment, and then he snapped his fingers. "I've got it. I'm going to buy something special for the guys."

'The guys' he was referring to were Emily's mascots, three stuffed animals she'd adored since childhood, even going so far as to naming her little newsstand after them: Cow, Spots, and Moose. "You know, that just might work."

"It's better than that. I had the distinct impression that Dusty wasn't a true believer in the reality of the guys. That's a death knell in Emily's heart; there's no doubt about that."

I had to laugh. "It doesn't sound like you need my help after all. Any idea what you might get them?"

"I'm not sure," he said with a slight frown. "They have just about everything a stuffed animal could ever want. Over the years, Emily's bought them dozens of props to go with the outfits that she's made them."

"Well, think about it. What haven't they dressed up as yet that she would love? You need to go through the scrapbook of photos she's taken of them over the years."

"I've just about got that thing memorized," he said. "It's a pretty complete album of photographs."

I patted his shoulder. "Don't worry. I'm sure that you'll come up with something. I'm really sorry, but I need to take off."

"That's fine," he said absentmindedly. "Thanks again for the advice."

"Happy to help," I said as I started to get into the Jeep.

Max was walking away when I suddenly had a thought. "Max, I might have something for you."

He hurried back to me. "Great. What have you got?"

"National Donut Day is the first Friday in June. Why don't you dress them up as chefs and have a celebration?"

"They've already worn those outfits," he said with a

sigh.

"How about commissioning someone to make them all costumes so that they can be donuts themselves, then? Emily would get a kick out of that, and I'll make you a dozen red-iced donuts to take her instead of roses."

"Do you think she'd go for that?" he asked.

"It couldn't hurt. I'm just not sure who you can get to make the costumes, though."

"I've got that part covered," he said with a smile. "Hillary Teal makes the outfits for our stage productions in our amateur theatre group, so I bet that she'd be willing to do it."

I knew that Max had enjoyed directing our seniors in productions targeted for much younger actors, much to the town's delight. Hillary, along with a host of other men and women of a certain age, enjoyed everything from acting, prop making, and sewing. "That's perfect."

"Thanks for the idea," he said.

"Happy to help."

As I drove to the bank, I just wished that all of my problems were that easy to solve, not that I thought Max had anything to worry about. When Dusty had left town, it was no secret that he'd been more in love with himself than anyone had a right to be, and my ex was devoted to Emily. Still, it wouldn't hurt if he showed her how he felt, and Max had been dead-on about one thing: the way to Emily's heart definitely was through her three mascots and best friends, Cow, Spots, and Moose.

My nap wasn't a long one, but at least it was something, so I was ready before Grace came around to the cottage so we could start our sleuthing. By the time she got there, I had awakened to an empty house, showered, and changed into fresh clothes. As much as I loved making donuts, they definitely left a distinct aura around me until I could wash it off. Jake claimed to love the scent, but part of me suspected that he was just indulging me. Then again, I'd had a friend once who'd fried a pound of bacon before every date just for the scent of it on her, and she had a line of boyfriends longer than any one girl could manage. Everyone else had thought it was a joke, but she had clearly known what she was doing. Me, I just relied on my charm and wit, but if the aroma of donuts really was attractive to Jake, I wasn't going to dissuade him. However, today was about the investigation that Grace and I were about to take up, so I needed to feel as though I had a clean start before we started interviewing our suspects.

"Good, you're awake," Grace said after I answered her knock on the cottage front door.

"Why wouldn't I be?" I asked her with a smile.

"I was afraid that today might have worn you out completely."

"It did, but I managed to squeeze in a quick nap and a shower, so I'm as good as new."

Grace nodded. "Perfect. I finished up early, so we can get started. Who are we going after first?"

"Let me grab my keys and we'll talk about it on the way." I locked the door behind me, and as we made our way out to the Jeep, I said, "I have three thoughts for today."

"I can't wait to hear them," she said.

"We should go see Conrad Swoop, Violet Frasier, and then we can snoop around Evelyn's place to see if we can uncover something that the April Springs police might have missed."

"Do you think there's a chance we'll stumble across anything if Jake has investigated the scene himself?" she asked me.

"I don't know, but it's got to be worth a shot. After all, we have an advantage over him."

"I'd love to hear what that might be," Grace said as she got into the passenger side.

As I got in and started the Jeep, I said, "We know how women think."

"Is that going to be enough?" Grace asked.

"I don't know, but it has to be worth something, don't you think? Since Conrad and Violet are both in Union Square, I thought we might stop by Evelyn's place first on our way out of town."

"How exactly are we supposed to get inside?"

"Knowing Evelyn, there's bound to be a spare key hidden somewhere around the property."

"And if there's not?" she asked me.

"Then we improvise."

"I'm not opposed to breaking into her place if we can't find a key, but I'm pretty sure that Jake's not going to be pleased if he finds out about it."

"Then it's important to make sure that he doesn't find out, isn't it?" I asked her with a grin.

"I like the way you think," Grace said as I drove away from the cottage and headed straight to Evelyn's home. If we got lucky, we just might be able to find a clue that could lead us directly to whoever killed her.

"Why isn't there any crime scene tape on her door?" Grace asked me when we got to Evelyn Martin's house.

"She wasn't killed here, remember?" I parked the Jeep twenty feet past her house and on the opposite side of where Robby Chastain lived. I didn't want Robby to see us snooping at Evelyn's, especially since we'd already talked to him. If he hadn't been suspicious of us before, seeing us lurk around the murder victim's home would surely do it.

"Of course she wasn't," Grace said. "I still figured that Jake would make the place off-limits."

"Maybe he's already checked it out," I said as I turned off the engine and got out.

Grace followed me outside. "Hasn't he told you?"

"Believe it or not, we don't discuss every development

in the case."

"At least that makes one of you," she said.

"What do you mean by that?"

Grace just shrugged. "I didn't mean anything by it. All I'm saying is that you have to tell him everything that we're up to, but he doesn't have to reciprocate."

"Hey, I'm just happy he hasn't banned us from investigating altogether," I said. "We're lucky he's being so lenient with us."

"I know, but I can't help wishing that somebody would take us into their confidence just once, you know what I mean?"

"Believe me, I get it," I said, "but we have to go with what we've got. Since Jake is working the case officially, we pretty much have to do what he says."

"How very unlike us," Grace said with a smile.

"At least we're not rolling over completely," I said. "After all, we're here, aren't we?"

"We are," Grace said as we approached the front door. She frowned when we got there, though. "I'm not exactly sure what we're going to be able to do about it, though."

"Let's see what we can find," I said as I ran my hand over the door trim. I knew that most folks liked to hide their spare keys in the most obvious places, including the doorjamb.

No luck there, though.

"Why don't you check under the Welcome mat?" Grace asked, obviously joking.

I stuck my tongue out at her as I leaned over and lifted one edge of the mat off the concrete.

"There's no key there, either. It appears that Evelyn was prepared to outfox anyone as savvy as we are. Maybe she didn't even leave a spare outside."

"It's possible, but I'm not finished looking yet," I said. There were some stones by the front door, so I started checking a few of those to see if there were any fake ones hiding among the real rocks. There weren't, and we still hadn't had any luck after five full minutes of searching. "How long are we going to keep this up?" Grace asked me. "The only reason I'm asking is that someone might notice that we're lingering outside an awfully long time."

"Let's give it another minute," I said as I approached a nearby flowerpot. I tilted the pot at an angle, but there was nothing underneath it.

Maybe it was hiding a little better there than that.

Sticking my fingers in the potting soil, I rooted around for anything that felt as though it might be a key.

"Really, Suzanne? Is that what this has come down to? Who sticks their spare key in the dirt?"

At that moment, my fingertip brushed a sharp point, and as I started to dig it out, I said, "Well, we've got Evelyn so far." I got a grip on the key and pulled it out. After cleaning it off as best as I could, I tried inserting it into the lock.

The front door opened with ease.

But we weren't home free, yet.

Something started beeping the second we opened the door.

Evidently Evelyn had an alarm system, something that I hadn't looked for before I'd unlocked the door.

"Let's get out of here," Grace said urgently. "We can't be here when it goes off!"

"I'm not ready to give up yet," I said. I stared at the keypad and noticed that the numbers 1, 5, 8, and 9 were the only numbers that were smudged and a little dirty. What could that mean?

"Suzanne, let's go!"

"Hang on. I've almost got it." I rearranged the numbers in my mind and punched in 1, 9, 5, and 8, holding my breath as I finished the last digit.

"Alarm Off," a voice said from the panel, and I finally let it out.

"How did you know the code?" my best friend asked in

clear bewilderment.

"I cheated," I admitted.

"How did you manage that?"

"Four numbers were a little more smudged than the others. I tried to figure out what the different sequences might be, and then I punched in what I'm guessing was Evelyn's birth year."

"Nice," Grace said. "You're pretty good at this, aren't you?"

"I have my moments, but don't forget, so do you."

"Now that we're inside," Grace said, "what do we do next?"

"We hunt for a clue as to who might have wanted to see Evelyn Martin dead," I said.

"Well, the house is barely the size of your cottage, so it shouldn't take that long to search," Grace said. "Do you want the master bedroom or the den and the kitchen?"

"I'll take the bedroom," I said. "I don't know how much time we have, so we have to make this quick. If you find something interesting, don't take the time to bring it to me. Take a photo of it with your phone, and we can compare notes later."

"Got it," Grace said as she went into the kitchen. "Happy hunting."

"You, too," I said as I hurried into the master bedroom.

The place was neat, which surprised me. Knowing Evelyn, even on the periphery, hadn't led me to believe that she'd be particularly fastidious, but the bedroom was almost Spartan in its minimalism. One picture was on the dresser, and to my surprise, it was of her and Chief Martin on what had to have been their wedding day. It was an odd constant reminder from a couple who had divorced under less than amiable conditions. Max and I had gone through a similarly bad breakup, and I couldn't imagine having his picture anywhere in the cottage, let alone in my bedroom. I didn't have much time to analyze it, though. As I'd told Grace, we were on the clock. I took my own advice and snapped a quick photo of it with my phone, then I decided that it was time to move on. The closet, where I'd had high hopes, turned out to be a bust, or so I thought until I searched the jacket pocket of a blazer hanging in back. Inside it, I found a small box and wrapping. Inside that was a gold necklace, obviously not all that expensive to my eye, and a small card that said, "To Evie. Love, Connie." No doubt that was Conrad Swoop, her new significant other. How significant could he really be, though, with the photo of her and the chief out there for all of the world to see? She hadn't exactly deemed the necklace as being all that important, or it wouldn't have still been in her jacket pocket. I considered taking the necklace to show Grace, but in the end, I decided to keep that information for later. I took a few more shots and then put everything back where I'd found it.

Her nightstand was a little more yielding. Inside it, I found more notes from Connie, but more significantly, buried in the pile was one from Violet Frasier. She'd written a short but nasty note telling Evelyn to drop Conrad, or there would be consequences. It sounded a little desperate to me, so I was careful to get a good shot of it as well. I decided to check the trash, and I found something interesting there. Buried under a few papers, I found a belated birthday card from Julie Gray. Not only had Evelyn thrown it away, but she'd torn it in half first. That was a significant statement in and of itself, so I took a photo of the torn card and tried to put it back just like I'd found it. That left her dresser, after I carefully examined Evelyn's bed, between the mattress and the box springs, and even under it. Nothing. In the dresser, I found something that looked like a date book. Had it been possible that Jake or one of his temporary team members had missed this? Flipping through it, I saw a few interesting facts scrawled inside it. One was about a meeting she was supposed to have with her attorney for

that very day. It wasn't the one she'd mentioned to
Momma, either, so this lawyer had to be about something
besides the partnership. Flipping through the other
pages, I also found a notation that she would be meeting
with the chief himself in a few days. Why hadn't he
mentioned that to anyone? Did Momma even know?
How about Jake? It raised more questions than I could
answer, so I decided to take another photo and then I
returned it to the drawer. I looked around the room, and
if there was another possible clue hiding anywhere in
there, I'd missed it. It was time to see if Grace had any
more luck than I had.

"Were you able to find anything?" I asked as I joined
her.

Grace was so startled, she looked as though she'd just
seen a ghost. "Don't sneak up on me like that," she said
as she held her heart. "You just about scared the life out
of me."

"Sorry, I'll try not to be so stealthy in the future."

"I'd appreciate that," she said with a wry smile. "Did
you have any luck?"

"I found a few little tidbits," I said. "How about you?"

"Nothing. Zilch. Nada."

"Then let's tackle the rest of the house together," I said
as I heard a key go in the front door lock.

"What do we do?" Grace hissed at me.

"We run," I said as I headed for the back door.

As Grace went through, I slid the locking mechanism
on the knob to lock automatically, but the door alarm
pinged as the door opened. Had the person coming in
heard it? I hoped not, but I didn't exactly have any time
to hang around and quiz them about it. If they noticed
that the alarm had been disabled, that was just too bad.
At least there hadn't been any security cameras inside.
Not that we'd seen, anyway. If we'd been captured on
film, I'd have to figure out a way to talk myself out of the
trouble, but until then, I wasn't going to worry about it.

Grace was waiting in the bushes for me as the door closed, and I hurried toward her. "Let's go," I whispered fiercely.

"I want to see who's in there," she said.

"We can't afford to be caught anywhere near here, remember?"

"Let's hang around for a few seconds. This could be important," she said, so I had a decision to make. Should I follow my own instincts and run for the next-door neighbor's yard and escape, or should I join Grace and share her fate, no matter what that might be? In the end, it wasn't really a decision at all. If my best friend was going down, then I was going, too. I ducked into the shrubbery with her and poked my head over the top so that I could see inside.

It took a moment or two for the person who'd gone in to show themselves, but when they finally did, I knew that Grace had been right to stay. I had to admit that it kind of shocked me to see who was there, though.

Who would have thought that Chief Martin would be doing a little breaking and entering himself after all of the times that he'd told me that I shouldn't be doing it?

Chapter 13

"What do we do?" Grace asked in a whisper. "Should we barge in and see what he's up to, do we call Jake, or do we leave and pretend that this never happened?"

"I don't know," I said, whispering back. "None of those options sound like good ones to me."

"Well, we don't have much time," Grace said. "We don't know how long the chief's planning to stay in there."

"Let's give him a minute and see what he does," I urged.

"You're the one who wanted to run away in the first place, remember?"

"That was before I knew that the burglar was our police chief," I replied. We watched as he walked over to the kitchen, peered into a few cabinets, and then headed off toward Evelyn's bedroom. "Let's go."

"Are we honestly going to just leave without seeing what he's up to?" Grace asked me.

"No, we're going to see if we can get a better look through the window in there," I answered.

"Now you're talking," Grace said.

We hurried over to the bedroom window and tried to peek inside. Only a part of the shade was pulled, so it was tougher to see in there, but when I looked through the glass, I saw the chief holding the framed photo of him and his late wife on their wedding day. Was it purely sentimental? I thought so at first, but then I saw him turn the frame over and quickly remove the back of it. I'd never thought of searching there for anything! As Chief Martin took the backing off, something fluttered to the floor, but I couldn't see what it was. I had been within inches of that frame just moments ago, not to mention whatever clue that might be hiding there, but I hadn't been smart enough to look behind the picture.

What could it be?

I was about to ask Grace her opinion when I glanced over at her and saw something that made the question die in my throat before I even had a chance to ask it.

Evidently our breaking and entering hadn't gone unnoticed after all.

Someone was standing at the corner of the house, staring at us with the most disapproving expression that I'd ever seen in my life.

Grace must have seen my face at the instant I spotted our unwelcome guest.

"What's wrong?" she asked.

All I had to do was point.

"Ladies, what are you up to now?"

It was a question I wasn't really prepared to answer, especially not to the person asking.

Chapter 14

"Shh," I said softly to Jake. "Creep on over here. You're going to want to see this."

"I'm not going to skulk around in the bushes," he said in his normal voice. "I asked you a question, and I expect an answer."

"We're watching Chief Martin," I whispered as I gestured inside.

Jake looked surprised by the news. He frowned as he asked us, "The chief's inside? He shouldn't be in there."

As he disappeared around toward the front of the house, I grabbed Grace's arm. "Come on. We need to see this."

Jake was at the front door by the time we got there. I was going to tell him about the key, and the alarm, but I wanted to wait and see what happened first. There was no reason to admit to what we'd done earlier if we didn't have to.

The front door was unlocked when he tested it, and I tried not to let the relief show on my face.

"Stay here," he commanded as he turned to us for a moment before going inside.

I wanted to follow him anyway, but after the way he'd ordered us to stay put, I knew instantly that this wasn't one of those times that I could afford to disobey him, not as Jake, but as the acting investigator in a murder case.

I didn't have to make a decision though, because the chief must have been ready to leave. Jake was two steps inside the house as Chief Martin was making his way out, so while we couldn't see the men as the conversation occurred, at least we could hear them.

"Chief, have you lost your mind? You know that you can't be here," Jake said plaintively. If his voice hadn't sounded so disappointed, I might have enjoyed the scolding nature of his tone.

"I'm sorry," Chief Martin said, the apology clear in his voice, as well as his words. "I had to come by. We were together for a long time."

"I know what it's like to lose someone you love," Jake said, and I thought yet again about his dead wife, and the unborn baby she'd been carrying the day of her car accident. It had wounded him to the core, and sometimes I wondered if he'd ever be able to fully move on and start a new life with me. It had taken him ages to confess that his wife had been pregnant when she'd died, and it had nearly killed Jake to finally fill me in on the details.

"I know enough to realize that you can't compare my situation to yours," the chief said. "Evelyn and I were divorced, but I still felt something toward her, you know? We had a lot of years together, and some of them weren't all that bad." It wasn't exactly a ringing endorsement of his first marriage, but at least it was believable.

"That still doesn't justify this behavior. Are you telling me that is the reason that you were here? You just came by to reminisce about old times? I'm not sure that I can buy that."

"Well, I also thought I might be able to find something that you might have missed."

Jake's tone was clear disapproval now. "Why am I not surprised? I haven't even had a chance to thoroughly search the place myself, but a few of your people have already been and gone. So, did you find anything?"

"Nothing," the chief said, and I knew that he was lying.

I didn't even hesitate, though saying something now was clearly going to cause me some trouble down the road. "That's not entirely true," I said.

Grace looked at me with her mouth agape. She whispered, "You just ratted out your stepfather to the state police."

"No, I told Jake something that he needed to know for his ongoing investigation," I answered.

"It's the same thing."

"Maybe so," I said as Jake and the chief stepped outside. "But I didn't really have any choice, did I?"

"What's this about?" Jake asked me with a furrowed brow.

The chief was staring at me with bullets in his gaze, but I wasn't about to back down. "We saw him take something from the back of their wedding photo."

"How could you possibly know that, unless you were spying on me?" the chief asked me.

"Hey, don't try to turn this around on us. You're the one who was inside when you weren't supposed to be, not Grace and me." I couldn't rightfully take the moral high ground, but neither man knew that, and I was pretty sure that Grace wouldn't set them straight.

Jake looked long and hard at the chief before he spoke. "Is what Suzanne just said true?"

Chief Martin nodded, and then he reluctantly reached into his shirt pocket and pulled something out of it. "This has nothing to do with the case. It's just something that has some sentimental value to me, that's all."

I could see that it was an old-style hundred-dollar bill when he handed it to Jake. Could that have been what had fallen to the floor? I couldn't be sure, since I hadn't had a good view of it at the time. I supposed that it was possible, but was it the truth?

"Is that what you saw him take?" Jake asked me.

"I'm not sure," I admitted. "Grace?"

"I didn't see it," she said.

"How is this significant to you?" Jake asked the chief as he held the bill up.

"My mother gave us that hundred on our wedding day to put aside for a special occasion. We never touched it through the years, and I never expected to find it still there in the back of the picture frame, but when I opened it, sure enough, there it was. Like I said, it was strictly sentimental."

"I'm sorry, but you know that I'm going to have to

Custard Crime   108   Jessica Beck

keep this for now," Jake said as he put the money into an
evidence bag he pulled from his pants pocket.

"I know the drill," the chief said as he frowned.
"Technically, it wasn't mine anymore, anyway. I should
have gotten it back before we divorced, but I was so
relieved for the marriage to be over that I forgot all about
it."

"That still didn't make taking it right," Jake said.

"Hey, take it easy on him," I said, surprising myself
coming to the police chief's defense. "He explained why
he took it."

"Suzanne, I'll deal with you later."

"What did I do?" I asked him in a voice as innocent as I
could muster. In my mind, I added the phrase, "that you
know of," but I kept that part to myself.

"You were snooping around where you didn't belong,"
the chief said.

"Hey, I just took your side, remember?" I asked.

"After you told on me," Chief Martin said grimly. He
turned to Jake and asked, "Am I free to go, or are you
going to arrest me for trespassing?"

"If you come back here again without my knowledge or
permission, that's exactly what I'm going to do."

"But for now?"

Jake showed the hint of a grin as he said, "The door
was open when you got here, and you thought you heard
someone in trouble inside. As the police chief for April
Springs, it was your duty to investigate."

Chief Martin laughed for a moment. "And the bill I
just gave you?"

"The way I see it, you were turning over some evidence
you found to the proper authorities. There's nothing
illegal about that, either, is there?"

"Thanks, Jake," the chief said somberly. "I don't know
what I was thinking coming over here like this."

He put a hand on Chief Martin's shoulder. "I know
that this has to be tough on you, but you have to let me

handle this, Phillip."

"Okay," the chief said. I looked around, and I noticed that he hadn't parked anywhere near Evelyn's house, either. As he started to walk away, I stepped in front of him. "I'm sorry. Whether I should have done that or not, Jake needed to know."

"And your boyfriend takes precedence over me. I get it," Chief Martin said, though there was more sadness than ire in his voice. "I can see where you're coming from, but what happened to looking after family? Or don't you think of me as being a part of yours now, even after I married your mother?"

"I'll tell you the same thing that I once told Grace. If I ever had evidence that she did something she shouldn't have, I'd turn her in, and then I'd find her the best lawyer that I could, and she's the closest thing to family besides my mother and father that I've ever had."

"It's true," Grace said with a smile. "Suzanne here has a really warped sense of right and wrong. It's an impossibly high standard to live up to."

"I like to think that it's exactly what it should be," I said.

"Fine. Whatever," the chief said as he walked away. I had some serious fences to mend with the man, but none of it would be done right now.

"As for you two," Jake said as he locked the door behind him, "I'm not sure what to do with you."

"A neat shiny medal would be nice," Grace said, "or maybe you could name us crime-busters of the month or something."

"Grace, this is serious," he told my best friend, though I could see the ghost of a smile forming on his face.

"In the end, what did we really do?" she asked him. "We reported a possible crime to the police. How is that a bad thing, Jake?"

"You were here snooping around and you happened to catch the chief doing something that he shouldn't have been doing, either. How does that make you two any better than him?"

"Hey, we didn't take anything," Grace said.

"That I know of," Jake replied.

It was time to defuse this situation. "Listen, for what it's worth, telling you about that potential clue cost me something with the chief and with my mother. I didn't try to protect anyone. That should count in our favor, at least."

"It does," Jake admitted. "It's just that I'm not used to having my investigations hijacked like this."

"We're facilitators, not interferers," Grace said with a smile. "It might help if you thought of us as assets and not liabilities."

"How I wish that I could," Jake said with a wry smile. "Where are you two troublemakers off to now?"

"We thought we'd have chats with Conrad and Violet," I readily admitted to him.

"Tread lightly, okay?" Jake asked.

I couldn't believe he was going to let us go ahead with our plans. Was he going to use us to soften them up, or had he already spoken with them and struck out? Whatever the case was, I wasn't about to complain about it. "We will," I replied. "What are you going to do now?"

Instead of answering, Jake just smiled at me, and then he saluted us both before he walked to his squad car.

After he was gone, Grace said, "Well, that certainly worked out better than either one of us had any right to expect."

"What makes you think that part of it is over?" I asked her just as my cellphone rang.

No surprise, it was my mother, and I was certain she wasn't calling to inquire about my general health.

"Hello, Momma," I said when I answered the phone.

"Suzanne, you need to accept this marriage between

Phillip and me, do you understand? I thought we were already past this juvenile behavior, but now I've learned that's not the case at all."

"He started it," I said in childish protest, probably a little ill-advised at the moment.

"Suzanne, this is not the time for your questionable sense of humor."

"Momma, I'm sorry that I ratted your husband out to Jake, but I thought that there might be a real chance that he was hiding something. In my defense, when Jake asked him if he'd found anything, the chief denied it to his face, even though I knew better. What choice did I have?"

"Phillip told you the rationale for his behavior," she said.

"I'm sorry, but when he withheld the truth, all bets were off as far as I was concerned. Besides, he told Jake about it after I confronted him, so where's the harm?"

"The harm is that you may have done irreparable damage to your relationship with your stepfather."

That kind of burned me up, and the filter that told me to keep my mouth shut was clearly not working at the moment. "Just because he's your husband doesn't make him my stepfather." I regretted the words the moment they escaped my lips, but there was no getting them back now. "I'm sorry. I didn't mean it to sound so harsh, but that doesn't mean that it's not true."

"Nevertheless, the sentiment clearly expressed how you truly feel. We'll talk later," she said.

"Hang on. Don't hang up." But it was too late.

Momma had already broken the connection, and I knew better than to call her back, at least not until I gave us both time to collect ourselves. Could I bring myself to apologize? What I'd said was true enough. The chief was her husband, and I was fine with that, but I wasn't sure that I'd ever be able to embrace him as my stepfather. It wasn't like I was eleven years old. I was a grown woman, divorced myself, for goodness sake. So why did I feel so awful for how I'd just behaved, no matter how justified I felt?

"Wow, that was really ugly," Grace said as she stroked my arm lightly. "Are you okay?"

"I've been better," I said. "I'm going to have to find a way to make things right, but now is not the time. We have a case to investigate."

"Are you sure that you shouldn't go to your mother's right now and try to resolve this between you? Isn't sooner better than later?"

"Not in this case. Come on. Let's forget about my mother and her husband and focus on Evelyn's murder. Who should we tackle first, Conrad or Violet?"

"I say we talk to good old Connie," Grace said.

"Any reason in particular?" I asked her as we headed back to where we'd parked the Jeep.

"Just call it a hunch," Grace said.

"That's good enough for me," I said.

As we drove to Union Square, it was time to bring Grace up to date about what I'd found in Evelyn's house during our search before we'd been interrupted by the police chief's unexpected visit.

I handed her my cellphone.

"Do you want me to call someone for you?" Grace asked, looking a little confused.

"No. Look at the most recent photos I took," I suggested.

"Suzanne, I don't want to see pictures of donuts you'd made again."

"That was one time," I protested, "and I was trying to get your opinion on an icing color. I'm talking about some shots I took inside Evelyn's that you might be interested in."

"Now you're talking," she said as she pulled up my most recent shots. After studying the entries in Evelyn's appointment book, Grace asked, "What's this supposed to be?"

I glanced at it, but I didn't feel all that comfortable about taking my eyes off the road. "Let me pull over and check," I said. I found a spot where it was safe, pulled over, and then I took the phone from Grace. "Okay, if we turn it this way and I tap the screen once, it might be a little clearer." The note from Violet showed up legibly when I did that, so I handed the phone back to Grace.

"Wow, is it just me, or is Violet a little bat-crap crazy?"

"It's not just you," I said as I moved to another picture. "This one is from Conrad," I said as I showed her the shot of the necklace and card.

"It's not all that nice a necklace, is it?" Grace asked as she studied the image displayed.

"How can you tell just by looking at a picture of it on a cellphone?"

"Hey, I've trained myself in distinguishing the finer things," she said. "Where did you find this?"

"In one of her jacket pockets," I said.

"So, it clearly didn't mean much to Evelyn, either."

"What makes you say that?"

"It never even made it into her jewelry box," Grace said. "What else do you have?"

"How about this?" I asked as I reached over and flipped to the final relevant photo, the one of the torn birthday card from her cousin, Julie.

Grace glanced at it. "Where did you find this?"

"In the trashcan," I said.

"And was it in one piece when you discovered it there?"

"Actually, it was ripped in half," I said.

"So, Julie was out of favor with Evelyn when she was murdered."

"I think that it's safe to assume that. What does it mean, though?"

"That we have more digging to do, but at least we have

some ammo now. I'm sorry to say that I didn't find anything during my part of our search."

"I'm not surprised. After all, you got the toughest area."

"At least we've got these," she said.

As I pulled back out onto the road, Grace and I started chatting about the best ways to approach our suspects, but we still hadn't been able to come up with anything spectacular by the time we pulled into Union Square. As usual, it appeared that we'd be playing this one by ear.

It was probably for the best. Grace and I were never all that great at outlining our plans. We usually believed that operating by the seats of our pants was the best way to investigate. Normally, all that a preset idea did was lock us into a particular course of action, whether it was the best way to move forward or not. When we ad-libbed things, we were much more capable of going wherever the investigation led us instead of clinging to any preconceived notions we might be going in with.

At the moment, our plan was to have no plan at all, an oxymoron if ever there was one.

Chapter 15

"You must be Connie Swoop," I said as I extended a hand to the man we were looking for when Grace and I walked onto a car lot in Union Square. He matched the description I'd been given to a tee, down to the carefully styled but unnaturally tinted brown hair, the slick business suit, and a pair of dress shoes sporting an impossible shine.

It was clear that he wasn't all that thrilled with the nickname, but he was too good a salesman to get too upset about it. "Actually, it's Conrad," he said through a set of overly brightened teeth. "And you two lovely ladies are?"

I decided to ignore his question and follow up with one of my own. I'd seen politicians do it often enough, so how hard could it be? "Really? You don't like that? Funny, I could have sworn that I heard it was Connie. At least that's how Evelyn Martin always referred to you."

His features hardened for a split second before he recovered his aplomb. "Were you friends with Evelyn? It was tragic, the accident that happened to her."

"It was no accident," Grace said, "or hadn't you heard?"

Conrad pretended to falter, but I didn't believe it. He stuttered out, "Are you saying that someone pushed her on purpose?"

"That's the prevailing theory," I said. "When's the last time that you saw her, Conrad?" I made sure to emphasize the name as I said it.

The salesman frowned for a moment before answering. "It had to be three days ago. We were going to go out to dinner, but I'm sorry to say that we were interrupted before we could really get started."

"What happened?" Grace asked.

"A woman that I see occasionally somehow got the

wrong impression about our relationship, and she confronted me at my home while Evelyn was visiting."

"What was her name?" Grace asked.

"I don't believe that's any of your business," he answered.

"I'm guessing it was Violet Frasier. Am I right?" I asked.

"Bingo." Wow, he gave that up pretty quickly. The real question was, was he being helpful, or was he trying to get us distracted before we could focus too hard on him?

"We plan to talk to her as well," I said, "but since we're here speaking with you, we'd like to know where you were yesterday morning. If you were working here, I'm sure that someone can alibi you."

"Yesterday was my day off," he said. "I spent it driving in the mountains."

"Alone?" I asked.

"Yes," he said, clearly getting irritated with our line of questions. "Who exactly are you?"

It was time to tell him. "I'm Suzanne Hart," I said, "and this is my best friend, Grace Gauge."

"I didn't *think* that you two were with law enforcement," Conrad said a little disdainfully. "What business is it of yours where I was?"

"We had close ties with Evelyn," I said. It was stretching the truth, but Conrad didn't know that.

"Funny, she never mentioned either one of you to me."

"Maybe she just forgot, like you forgot to tell Violet and Evelyn about each other. Neither one of them knew that you were dating the other one, did they? You said that Violet was upset, but I'm pretty sure that Evelyn wasn't all that pleased about it when she found out, either."

"She understood, once I explained the situation to her."

"Is that why you bought her that cheap gold necklace?" I asked, playing a hunch. "Were you trying to make it up to her?"

Conrad looked sharply at me. "How did you know about that?"

"I told you that we were close, remember?"

"That necklace was given out of love and affection, nothing more."

"Did you happen to give a duplicate one to Violet?" Grace asked. It was a question that wouldn't have even occurred to me to ask, but I was glad that she'd thought of it. One look at Conrad's face told me that she'd scored a direct hit.

"That's nobody's business," he said brusquely. "Now, unless one of you is here looking for a new vehicle, I'd appreciate it if you'd move on."

"Who knows?" I asked. "I might replace my Jeep soon." To anyone who knew me, it was clearly a lie. I was as devoted to that vehicle as I was to my friends and family. Well, not quite that much, but it was still pretty close.

"What were you looking to spend?" he asked. "We've got a lovely little Subaru with low miles on it that you might like. Why don't we take it for a spin?"

There was no way I was getting into a car with this guy, with or without Grace, and I had a hunch he wouldn't let me take it out on my own, even if I had been serious about buying it.

"Sorry, but I need to trust the man I'll be working with first," I said. "Are you trustworthy, Conrad?"

"Ask just about anybody," he said. "I'm a man of principle, and my word is my bond."

"If that's true, then why didn't you pay Evelyn back the money that she loaned you?" Grace asked him sweetly.

He frowned again. "I don't know where you're getting your information from, but I paid Evelyn back every penny I borrowed from her, with interest."

"When did this supposedly happen?" I asked him.

"Last week."

"Can you prove that?" Grace asked him.

"I don't have to, not to you, and not to the police."

"I don't know, Connie," Grace said as she shook her head sadly. "It sounds as though there's nobody to dispute your version of what happened but Evelyn, and unless we hold a séance, she's not going to be telling her side of the story."

"That's it," Conrad said angrily. "You're obviously not looking for a car, and what's worse, you're trying to pin whatever happened to Evelyn on me. Well, I'm not going to stand here and take it. You both need to leave."

"Or what?" I asked him.

"Or you'll regret it," he answered in a tone of voice that chilled my blood.

Either Conrad Swoop was bluffing, or he was about to commit an act of violence against my best friend and me. All I knew was that it wasn't the right time to find out which plan he had in mind. "Come on, Grace. Let's go."

"But we're not finished with him, yet," she said.

"We are for now," I answered.

"For good," he replied.

"Sorry, but that's not going to happen," I said. "Until we discover who killed Evelyn Martin, we're not giving up."

Once we were back in the Jeep, Grace asked, "Did you see that guy's face when I started pressing him? He was seriously upset with me."

"With us," I amended. "He's got a real temper, doesn't he?"

"He could have done it," Grace said matter-of-factly.

"Maybe, but being a hothead isn't enough proof one way or the other. I wonder if it's gotten him into trouble in the past?"

"There's only one way to find out," Grace said. "Put that phone of yours to good use."

"I'm not calling Jake, and I won't ask Chief Martin."

Grace frowned, and then she said, "Well, if you won't talk to either one of them, we still have one other cop in our arsenal."

"Are you talking about Stephen?" Officer Grant might be her boyfriend, but I doubted that he'd help us if it could cause trouble for him at work.

"No, we're not about to drag *him* into this. I was thinking more along the lines of George. After all, he used to be a cop, and it's not as though he hasn't helped us in our investigations in the past."

"True, but he wasn't the mayor of April Springs then."

"Maybe not, but you know he'd help us if we asked him. What can it hurt?"

"Grace, what if it comes back to haunt him later when he's running for mayor again? Could you live with the idea that he lost because of us?"

"Suzanne, you know as well as I do that everybody loves him in town. He's going to win reelection again in a landslide."

"Maybe," I said. "But let's put that particular inquiry on the back burner for now, okay?"

"Fine. Does that mean that it's time to tackle Violet Frasier? I wonder if she's as crazy as everyone says she is?"

"There's only one way to find out," I said as I started driving in the direction of where her house stood.

"Go away," the middle-aged woman said as we neared her front porch. I suppose some people would call her pretty, in an odd sort of way. For one thing, her eyes were spaced too close together, and they had too intense a look about them for my taste. She'd opened her front door just wide enough to stick her head out and warn us off.

"Violet, we just want a moment of your time," Grace said.

"Can't you read the sign? It says no soliciting, and that

includes any reason you think you might have for coming to my house."

"We're not here to sell you anything," I said hastily. "We're here to talk about Conrad Swoop and Evelyn Martin."

Her gaze narrowed. "What makes you think that I want to talk about either one of those dirtbags?"

"Am I right in assuming that you aren't dating Conrad anymore?" I asked her.

"He was two-timing me with that Martin woman. What an idiot."

"Which one?" Grace asked.

"Take your pick," she said angrily. There was some real rage just below the surface.

"We already know that you weren't a fan of Evelyn's," I said. "We read your note threatening her."

Violet just laughed at the accusation. "So what? I didn't follow through with it. I thought I might be able to scare her off, but it didn't work."

"Well, someone certainly took care of her for you," I said.

Violet didn't look all that distressed about her rival's fate. "She fell through some floorboards. I'd hardly call that a conscious act of vengeance."

"It would be if she were pushed," Grace said.

That was news to her, or she was just trying to tone down the crazy in her. "Are you saying that somebody shoved her?"

"That's what it looks like to the police."

Violet shook her head, but as she did so, the ghost of a smile crossed her lips for a moment before she spoke. "Conrad told me that he'd warned her to stop coming around him, but I never thought the little weasel would ever really do anything about her."

"So, let me get this straight. You're telling us that Conrad was dumping Evelyn Martin for you, is that it?"

"Why is that so hard for you to believe?" Violet asked

as she ran a hand through her hair. "I'm an attractive woman."

"I'm not denying it," I said hurriedly. "It's just that what you're telling us doesn't match up with what Connie told us earlier."

"Don't call him that," she reproached me automatically. "He hates when people do that."

"That's how he addressed himself to Evelyn," I said.

"You're lying."

"I can prove it," I said as I pulled out my cellphone. "Would you care to see?"

I pulled up the photo of the necklace and card and showed it to her. Her face turned beet red, and I was worried that she might burst a blood vessel. "That complete and utter jerk."

"Did you get a necklace just like that one?" Grace asked.

"He must have gotten a bulk discount on them," she said as she shoved my phone away.

"I'm sorry," I said in earnest. "I probably shouldn't have shown you that."

Violet shook her head, and it was clear that she was fighting back tears. "No, I needed to see that for myself. Well, I can tell you one thing. He's lied to me for the last time."

"When else has he lied to you?" Grace asked gently.

"Don't get me started. I can't even count the times. Listen," she said as she wiped at her eyes. "I have to go."

"Can we just ask you one more thing?" Grace asked her.

"What is it?"

"Where were you when Evelyn died?"

Violet shook her head in disgust, and then she retreated back inside, slamming the door as she did.

"What can I say? It was worth a shot," Grace said.

"Maybe Jake will have more luck with her," I said.

"I kind of doubt it. She wasn't exactly cooperative

with us, and look how sympathetic we were to her."

"Jake has his own set of skills," I said. "Don't underestimate him."

"Hey, he managed to get you to fall in love again after your experience with Max. I'm not about to put anything past him if he can overcome the power of your first true love."

"Max wasn't my first love," I protested.

"Oh, sorry. I'm forgetting Tommy Thorndike in the sixth grade."

"What can I say? It was never meant to be, but it was glorious while it lasted."

She laughed at that, and I joined her.

"What should we do now?" Grace asked.

I looked at my watch, and saw that it was coming up on dinnertime soon. "If you don't mind, I'd like to get back to April Springs. I'm having dinner with Jake in about an hour."

"Why should I mind, especially since I'm going out with Stephen?"

"My, aren't we just two desirable young women," I said to her as we made our way back to my Jeep.

"That's what they all say," Grace replied. "How much of our afternoon's activities are you going to share with Jake?"

"Every last bit of them," I admitted. "I promised him that I would, and I'm not about to break my bond. You don't have any problem with that, do you?"

"Me? Not a chance. After all, I might just tell Stephen, too."

"Well, there's one good thing about this 'open book' policy. We don't have to keep any lies straight."

"What an odd experience that's going to be," Grace said with a laugh.

As we drove back to April Springs, we discussed the weather, our love lives, even my mother's new marital status, but one topic we resisted discussing was the murder case we were working on. Grace and I both knew that we needed a little time to let our minds play with what we'd uncovered so far. It was one of the reasons I loved investigating with her. We knew each other so well that we didn't have to explain ourselves to one another.

I didn't have long to digest our new information, anyway.

Soon enough, I'd be relaying every bit of it to Jake.

I just hoped that he decided to share some of what he knew with me, as well.

Chapter 16

"That's the last of the leftovers," I told Jake as we
finished eating our evening meal. Since he'd been shot,
folks had been supplying us with a steady stream of
offerings, but the donations had finally ended. I'd been
grateful for everything that we'd gotten, and it had
certainly helped out tremendously at mealtime, but I was
a little excited about cooking for Jake while he was still
in town, too.

"I hate to admit it, but I'm kind of happy about that,"
he said. "Not that I'm ungrateful."

"I was just thinking the same thing. How about some
homemade potato soup tomorrow night? I have a little
cheddar-chive bread left in the freezer."

"Was it a donation, too?"

"From Momma," I answered.

"Then I'm on board."

As I started clearing the table, Jake jumped up to help.
It was nice working together on something that wasn't a
homicide case. We'd agreed to postpone talking about
the investigation until after we ate, but it couldn't be
delayed any longer. "Should we talk about Evelyn while
we're washing dishes, or should we wait until later?"

"Why don't we do it now? I'm all for multitasking," he
said.

"Great. Do you want to go first, or should I?" I asked
him with a smile.

He returned my grin. "Nice try. Go on, I'm listening."

I brought him up to date on what Grace and I had
learned that day, not holding anything back. I'd made
him a promise, and I was determined to keep it, even if it
did feel really odd telling him everything I knew. Full
disclosure was an unsettling thing.

"What do you think at this point?" Jake asked me after
I was through with my recitation. "Have you come to

any conclusions so far?"

"It's still early," I said. "I hate to rush to judgment until I have more facts."

"Suzanne, I'm not asking you for an indictment. I'm just wondering what your gut is telling you."

That was fair. As I washed off one of the plates from dinner, I handed it to Jake, who rinsed it and put it in the drying rack. "Honestly, I'm still kind of torn at this point. There's something about Conrad Swoop that I don't trust. I know he's got the capacity to steal, but I'm not sure that he murdered Evelyn."

"What about Violet?"

"She might be a little unhinged, but if you're asking me if she's twisted enough to kill a rival, I'm not willing to say just yet," I replied.

"I suppose you'll say the same thing if I ask you about Beatrice and Robby, too, won't you?"

"Probably," I said as I handed him a glass to rinse. "You didn't mention Julie Gray, though. Did you forget about her, or have you eliminated her as a suspect?"

"She's still on my list, but that's where it gets complicated."

"How so?"

Jake took so long to answer that I was afraid he was going to ignore my question, but after a full minute, he finally said, "I know this is highly unusual, but I'm going to share some things with you that I probably shouldn't."

"Don't tell me anything that I can't tell Grace," I said firmly. "Even if it means that we flounder around in the dark, we'll do it together. I can't stand keeping secrets from her."

Jake nodded. "I admire your loyalty, but that complicates matters." He took another moment, and then he asked me, "If you swear her to secrecy, can you trust her not to share it with anyone else?"

"I trust Grace with my life," I said. "If I ask her, she'll do it."

"With no wavering?"

"None. You can take that to the bank."

Jake let out a sigh, and then he nodded. "Okay. I trust you, and because you trust Grace, I'm going to share a few things with you."

Before he could speak, I put a soapy hand on his arm. "Jake, please don't do anything that you might have trouble with philosophically. I know how important your job is to you, and I'd never ask you to compromise it for me."

Jake smiled, and then he patted my hand. "I appreciate that, but honestly, my job's lost some of its luster for me lately. I'm not at all sure that this is what I'm meant to be doing with the rest of my life."

"Does that opinion have anything to do with getting shot in the line of duty?" I asked him tenderly. I knew that his body had recovered from the wound, but I wasn't so sure about his spirit.

"Of course it does, but things have been building for some time. I can't keep hopping around the state investigating the worst crimes imaginable forever."

"I get that, but don't do anything rash just yet. You're still not over the shooting."

"That's true, but in a way, I'm not sure that I ever will be. I don't know, Suzanne. Sometimes I wish I had a quieter life, do you know what I mean?"

"I get it," I said. "There's a lot to be said for knowing what your day, your week, your month, even your year is going to be like."

"No offense, but I wouldn't want anything that predictable. I don't know how you do it."

"With a smile on my face and a song in my heart," I said, grinning.

"You know what I mean."

"I do. I'm the first one to admit that making donuts isn't for everyone, but it's perfect for me." I finished the last piece of silverware and handed it to him. "Let me ask you something. If you weren't a cop, what would you do with yourself?"

"Oh, I never said that I was tired of being a cop," Jake answered. "I just wish that I didn't deal with the worst of the worst all of the time. I wouldn't mind writing a parking ticket every now and then, you know what I mean?"

"That can be dangerous enough in and of itself," I said.

"Absolutely, but at least most times, nobody would be shooting at me." He rinsed the fork, dried it, and put it away. "Is that it?"

"Until we make more, that will do. Would you like some coffee?"

"That sounds nice," he said. "I can tell you what I found out today while you're making it."

"Are you sure?"

"I'm positive. I've had some time to think about it, and I agree with you. You and Grace could be a valuable resource to me. I'd be a fool not to use you."

"That's what I've been saying all along," I said as I tweaked his cheek.

"It just took me a little longer to get there," he admitted. "But I made it."

"That's all that's important in the end," I said as I filled the pot and flipped the switch. "Should we go out into the living room, or wait around in here?"

"The couch is more comfortable," Jake said as he rubbed his arm a little, the one where he'd been shot.

"Is your arm bothering you?"

"It's probably nothing. I get a twinge every now and then, but it goes away."

"Have you spoken with your doctor about it?"

"Suzanne, all that it probably means is that it's going to rain. Now, let's discuss the case. Honestly, I'm surprised that your mother hasn't already called you with the news herself."

A chill went through me. "How does this involve my

mother?"

"It doesn't, at least not directly. It's about Chief Martin."

"What about him?"

"Well, I'm not really sure what it means, but I just found out today that he was still the main beneficiary listed in Evelyn's will. Julie wasn't very happy about discovering it, I can tell you that."

"But she was so sure that she was inheriting everything," I said. "How did the chief react when you told him about it?"

"He seemed to be surprised enough to get the news," Jake said. "I have to give him credit. He knew right away what that meant for him."

"It makes him an even stronger suspect now, doesn't it?"

Jake nodded. "Not only that, but what was in Evelyn's appointment book gave me another lead."

I was a little disappointed that he'd found it, too. "Jake, why didn't your men take it with them when they found it? I thought you said that you hadn't searched the place yet?"

He grinned slyly at me. "I said that I hadn't *thoroughly* searched it, if you'll recall. Suzanne, you never asked me how I knew that Chief Martin was inside Evelyn's home today."

"Were you watching the house?" I asked, wondering if he'd seen Grace and me break in as well.

"No, I didn't have the time to do that, but I've had a few men go by the house on rotation, and one of them happened to see the chief going in as he was driving by."

"You left it there as bait, didn't you?" I asked, admiring Jake even more.

"Among other things," he admitted. "And look what I caught."

"So, what about the book gave you another clue?"

"Evelyn was meeting with an attorney about changing

her will," Jake said. "Julie was indeed set to inherit everything, but Evelyn never had a chance to implement her last wishes."

"Wow, that looks even worse for Chief Martin, doesn't it?"

"There's certainly one way of looking at it that strengthens the case against him," he admitted.

"You don't think he really did it, do you? Come on, Jake. You know the man. He's not a killer."

"Under ordinary circumstances I'd agree with you, but there's a great deal of money at stake here, and there was a known animosity between him and his ex-wife."

"That doesn't make him a killer," I said strongly.

"Of course it doesn't. Right now, though, it's just another piece of the puzzle to be considered." Jake rubbed my shoulder lightly. "Take it easy, Suzanne. Nobody's accusing anybody of doing anything just yet. Like you said, I'm just collecting information myself."

"Sorry. I guess I'm a little on edge when it comes to my mother's new husband."

"It's perfectly understandable," Jake said.

"Did you find anything else out today?" I asked him after the coffee was ready and we each had a mug.

"There was one more little tidbit that might prove useful later," he said.

"Can you tell me?"

"I can, but again, it has to be in the strictest of confidences."

"I've already given you my word," I said.

"I know. I just wanted to emphasize how important this is. We now have an eyewitness who saw Beatrice leaving the crime scene an hour before Evelyn's body was found."

"Wow, that's pretty bad for her, isn't it?"

Jake just shrugged. "She claims that it was all perfectly innocent, that Evelyn was fine when she left her, but as far as we know right now, she was the last person to see her business partner alive."

"Besides the killer, you mean," I said.

"Only if they aren't one and the same person," Jake replied.

"So, this isn't going to be as clear-cut as you thought at first, is it?"

Jake frowned. "That's turning out to be true enough."

"Why the frown? You've had tough cases before."

"I know, but my boss is already accusing me of dragging this out just so I can spend more time with you. He's regretting assigning me to the case already."

"What does the man expect from you, a miracle?"

Jake nodded. "That's exactly what he wants."

"In a way, it's your own fault. You know that, don't you?"

"How is that?"

"Well, if you weren't so good at what you did, he wouldn't keep getting these unrealistic expectations."

Jake laughed. "I suppose that's one way of looking at things."

"Hey, spinning a negative into a positive is what I do best," I said. I glanced at the clock and saw how late it was getting, not for normal folks, but certainly for anyone who worked in a donut shop. "I hate to do this, but I'm really beat. Getting back into the donut business was harder than I thought it would be."

"Don't apologize to me. I hope you sleep well."

I kissed him lightly, and then I smiled. "Don't stay up too late yourself. You have a big day tomorrow finding Evelyn's killer."

"Right back at you," he said as I walked up the steps to my room. It was wonderful having Jake with me, but I knew that it wasn't possible for it to last. If Momma's marriage and move had taught me nothing else, it was that things couldn't stay the way they were forever, and hoping otherwise was as useless as trying to make it snow with willpower alone.

Chapter 17

"This is your day today," I told Emma the next morning at the donut shop. "Why don't you get started on the cake donuts while I prep up front?"

My assistant smiled. "Let me get this straight. I can make whatever donuts I'd like, right?"

"Within reason," I said with a smile. "Our customers expect our regular menu, flavors like plain, chocolate, blueberry cake, etcetera."

"So then the answer is no, is that what you're saying?"

I was being too strict with her, and I knew it. What good would it do to let her make donuts her way if I controlled the types of donuts that she could make? "How about this? You can try one new recipe every week, and I won't say a word about it, no matter how outlandish it might sound to me. Is that fair?"

"Even if it's the new coffee-toffee combo I've been planning?"

It sounded dreadful to me, but what could it hurt to offer one odd donut every now and then? "That's fine, but just make two dozen, okay?"

"I can do that," she said. "Thanks for giving me this opportunity."

"Hey, as far as I'm concerned, you've more than earned it. Besides, it might be fun being on dish duty instead of being responsible for the entire day's output once in a while."

"You're still doing the yeast donuts though, right?"

"If you don't mind," I said. "I'd like to."

"That sounds great. This should break things up enough to keep things interesting for the both of us." As Emma started mixing batters for the various cake donuts we offered, I busied myself doing her early morning tasks like setting up the dining area and making sure all of the napkin holders were full. It felt so strange being out of the kitchen while I was at Donut Hearts, but it was important that I do this.

After I had everything ready, I walked back in to rejoin her.

"I hate to do this to you, but I'm just about to drop the first donuts," she said. "Do you mind going back up front?"

"No, it's fine," I said. The dropper we used was heavy, and I'd let it slip from my hands once, taking a nice chunk out of the wall. Since then, it had been store policy that whoever was not dropping donuts into the hot oil had to be out of firing range, just in case there was ever another slip, though it hadn't happened again in my tenure.

I walked back out front again and tried to figure out what I could do, but I'd already accomplished the tasks I'd had on my list. I found an old newspaper tucked under one of the couch cushions, so I opened the paper to see what Ray had to say about the small world we all lived in. If there was anything worse than reading old news, I wasn't sure what it might be. I was about to throw it in our recycling bin when there was a sudden tapping on the front door.

It was Robby Chastain!

I walked over to the door and said, "Sorry, but we're not open for hours yet."

"I'm not here for donuts. Suzanne, we need to talk."

I wasn't all that excited about speaking with one of our murder suspects alone, especially with Emma occupied in the back room. "Can't it wait until we open?"

"I guess so," Robby said, and then he started to walk off into the darkness.

I started regretting brushing him off immediately. Against my better judgment, I unlocked the front door and stepped outside. "I suppose I can give you two minutes, but then Emma's going to need me back inside."

"Thanks. I couldn't sleep because something's been

bothering me." He looked deep into my eyes as he added, "Suzanne, I know."

"Know what? Who killed Evelyn?" Was I about to get a solid lead in the case?

"No, I don't have a clue about that," he said dismissively, "but I saw you and Grace sneaking into Evelyn's house yesterday. I'm sorry, but I'm going to have to tell the police what I witnessed."

Were we actually going to be busted by a nosy neighbor after Grace and I had avoided Jake and the entire April Springs police force? Not if I could help it. "If you saw us, then you must have seen Chief Martin, and then Jake Bishop, the state police inspector, was there, too."

"Sorry. I must have missed them."

Of course he had. "Well, they were both there soon after Grace and I went in. We all had a discussion on the front porch not ten minutes after we all got there."

"I didn't know that. I had a phone call that I had to take," he said, sounding a little apologetic. "What were you doing there in the first place, Suzanne?"

I decided that the truth might be my best weapon right now. "I was looking for clues about who killed Evelyn."

"You're really going to try to solve this case yourself?"

"Along with some help from my friends, that's exactly what I'm going to try to do."

"I don't think that's a very smart move on your part," he said, watching me closely as he spoke.

That was what I'd initially been afraid of. "Robby, are you threatening me?"

"Of course not. I just think it's dangerous to get mixed up with killers."

"We'll be careful," I said.

"That's good, because you never know what's going to be around the next corner, do you?"

"You sure don't," I said. Even though Robby had said that he wasn't threatening me, it was still sounding like that to me. I was about to ask him something a little more pointed when the door to the donut shop opened behind me.

"Is everything all right out here?" Emma asked.

"It's fine," I said. "Robby just wanted to chat, but we're finished now, aren't we?" I asked him.

"Sure," he said. "You two have a good morning."

"You, too," I said, about as insincerely as he'd been.

"What was that all about?" Emma asked me as we walked back into Donut Hearts.

"Believe me, you don't want to know. Are the cake donuts finished already?"

"They've all been fried, glazed, and trayed," my assistant said, and then she added with a smile, "The first round of dishes are ready for you."

"That sounds great," I said.

"Suzanne, you really don't have to do them. I don't mind."

"Nonsense," I said as I started running hot water into the sink. "That was our deal. There's no way that I'm going to have you make the donuts and clean up, too. It's just not fair." I added some soap to the water and was immediately rewarded with bubbles forming. "Honestly, this might be kind of fun."

"Oh, yes, it's a real blast," she said. "What should I do while you're doing that?"

"Why don't you take a break? I can handle this, and then I'll get started on the yeast donuts."

"I could start them for you, if you'd like," Emma offered.

"Thanks, but I've got it," I answered as the first dirty bowl went into the water.

"If you're sure," she said, and then Emma walked out of the kitchen into the front.

There was a calm and peaceful rhythm to washing and then drying the bowls, measuring cups, and various utensils we used at the shop, and I found my mind drifting off to the murder case, and who might have done it. I'd read once that Agatha Christie had preferred doing dishes when working on the plots of some of her mysteries, and I could see why. It kept the body moving but freed the mind. Unfortunately, by the time I finished the first round of dishes, I was still no closer to solving Evelyn's murder than I had been when I'd started. At least I had a clean stack of dishes to show for it. With that done, it was time to start on the yeast donuts. Measuring out the ingredients into my large floor stand mixer, I flipped the switch and let things incorporate. After that, I removed the beater and covered the bowl to give the dough a chance to rest and raise, so I went out to tell Emma that it was time for our first break together.

To my surprise, I found her sound asleep on my favorite couch.

"Rise and shine, sleepyhead," I said with a smile as I swatted her lightly with a dish towel.

"Did I nod off?" she asked me as she sat up and rubbed her eyes.

"You did indeed. Are you ready for our break?"

"I thought I was just on one," Emma said as she stood and stretched.

"You were, but we can take this one together outside."

Once we were sitting at our table outside, Emma said, "To tell you the truth, I'm not sure that I like this new experiment."

"What's not to like?"

"I enjoy staying busy, and I like our routine. Can we go back to the old way?"

"Are you sure?" I asked her.

"I'm positive. I just have one request."

"What's that?"

"I still want to try one odd-flavored donut a week. It's not much trouble, and I'm still happy to do all of the dishes, but it's been fun creating new taste treats that might be raging successes or abysmal failures."

"You don't mind it when they don't work out?" I asked her.

"Are you kidding? I threw away more than my share of batter when Mom and I were running the place. In small quantities, of course."

"Of course. Sure, that sounds good to me. I like things done a certain way myself. I've got to tell you, though, washing dishes can be good for the spirit."

"Why do you think I don't mind doing them?" she asked me with a grin.

Too soon our timer went off, and our break was over. It was time to work on the yeast donuts again, and then get ready to serve our offerings to our customers. I was feeling better today than I had the day before, and I had a hunch that tomorrow would be even better. I was already getting back into the groove of donutmaking. I had really missed it while I'd been nursing Jake back to health. I wasn't as sure that I'd enjoy it once this murder was solved and Jake was back at his old job, though. I'd grown to relish his company since he'd come to the cottage to recover, and I knew that I'd miss him terribly once he was gone. With Momma across town, I'd be on my own for the first time in my life. Grace had managed it with style and aplomb for more years than I could count, but I was nowhere near as cool as my best friend was. I was certain that I would have a few sleepless nights before I got used to being in the cottage alone, but I knew that, given time, I'd be fine.

"Good morning, Mr. Mayor," I said as I unlocked the front door and opened for business. "You're not here to welcome me back again, are you? This is two mornings in a row, pretty unusual for you."

"As a matter of fact, I felt like a donut. I hope that's okay."

"You know that you're always welcome here," I said. "What's new in your world?"

"My job these days seems to consist entirely of shuffling papers, signing my name, and telling people they can't have what they want. You, on the other hand, get to see smiles all morning long from people you make happy. Want to trade?"

"Not on your life. It's not all peaches and cream here either, but I wouldn't take your job under gunpoint. You deserve more than one donut a day for doing it."

"Tell Polly that, would you?" he asked.

"Has she got you on a diet again?" His assistant—and girlfriend—was an enormously competent woman who was always on top of everything.

"Sort of. I can have one treat a day now, as long as it's within reason."

"I'm honored that you chose donuts for your treat twice in a row," I said.

"Hey, what can I say? I love your company, too."

"Right back at you," I said as I served him his standard fare.

George took a sip of coffee, and then he pointed to Emma's latest experiment. "Is it too late to change my mind about the donut I'm having?"

"No, that's fine," I said as I pulled the plain cake donut back. "What would you like instead?"

"How about one of those coffee-caramel creations?"

I got one for him, but as I slid the plate across the counter, I said in a low voice, "I should warn you, this is one of Emma's experiments."

"Have you tried one yet?" he asked me softly.

"I had a nibble," I said. "They're okay, but they're not my favorite."

"Perhaps I'll just have a taste then," he said as he pinched off a bite. "Just in case, let's keep my cake donut close by, okay?"

"You're the boss," I said. I glanced over my shoulder and saw that Emma was peeking out from the kitchen. "Careful. You're being watched," I said softly.

"I saw her," the mayor said softly, and then he took a healthy bite. "My, that's quite tasty."

"Easy there, don't overact," I whispered. "We don't want to give her the wrong idea."

"Who's acting?" he asked with a smile. "I really do like it." To prove his point, he took another big bite of Emma's creation, and then pushed the cake donut away from him. "That's an unexpected medley of tastes, isn't it? Can I have one for the road?"

"I thought that you were only supposed to have one," I said.

"Oh, it's not for me. I want Polly to try this for herself."

"I can do that," I said as I bagged one, pausing to give a thumbs-up to Emma first.

"Do you really like it?" I asked him softly as I took his money.

"It kind of grows on you after a second," George said with a grin. "Besides, I really want to see Polly's face when she tries it."

"You're too funny, Mr. Mayor," I said as I handed him his change. "Thanks for coming by. You always manage to brighten my day."

"I've often said the same thing about you, Suzanne. Promise me that you'll be careful, would you?"

"My job isn't exactly hazardous now that the donuts are all made."

"I'm not talking about your job; I'm talking about your hobby."

"Understood," I said.

"Jake doesn't mind you rooting around in his case?"

"What can I say? We've found a solid middle ground," I said.

"Good luck with that," George said, and he saluted Emma, and then he added a smile before he walked out of the donut shop.

Emma came out immediately after he was gone. "Did

he really get another one for later?"

"The other one was for Polly, but he really seemed to enjoy it."

She nodded. "Honestly, I thought it was a little too strong when I had one."

"Hey, you never know what folks are going to enjoy. At least we're giving them a reason to keep coming around, aren't we?"

"You know it. Well, I'd better get back to those dishes."

"I'll be right here," I said with a smile. I loved it when Emma was happy, and George's actions had really put a smile on her face. He was a nice man, a good guy, and a great mayor, and I was proud to call him my friend.

We were in a bit of a lull a few hours later when I was surprised to see Momma approaching the front door. Ordinarily my mother was not a huge donut fan, and I couldn't remember the last time I'd seen her in Donut Hearts. Was she still angry with me over our chat the day before? I decided to ignore it if she was.

"What a pleasant surprise," I said, adding my best smile when she walked inside. "Did you have a craving for donuts this morning, Momma?"

"Hello, Suzanne. Thank you for the offer, but I've already eaten breakfast. Do you have a moment to talk to me about something important?"

Well, that couldn't be good. "Sure, but can it wait? We're kind of busy right now." There were three customers in the shop at the moment, all of them quietly eating, and none of them were clamoring for my attention.

"I think Emma can manage for a few minutes without you," she said. "I wouldn't ask if it weren't important."

"Okay, let me just get her." I ducked out of the front and found Emma finishing up the latest round of dishes. "Hey, do you have a minute?"

"Sure, what's up?"

"I need you to cover the front for me."

Emma grinned at me. "Are you and Grace going to get started on your investigation early?"

"No, Momma's here, and she just told me that she wanted to talk."

"Ouch. That can't be good, can it?"

"I'm sure it's nothing," I said, hoping that I wasn't lying to her.

"You're probably right. Sure, I'd be glad to watch the counter."

I smiled at her. "You know, it wasn't all that long ago when you hated working the front."

"What can I say? I got used to it last month, and it turned out to be kind of fun. Most of our customers aren't that bad after all."

"I'm sure that they'd be relieved to hear that."

"Well, I'm not going to be the one who tells them," Emma said as she wiped her hands on a towel.

As we walked out front, I said, "Don't worry. This shouldn't take long."

"You don't have to rush on my account," she said. "Hey, there, Mrs. Hart. Or should I say Mrs. Martin?"

"It's still Hart," she said. "Hello, Emma. How are you?"

"Happy as can be, thanks for asking. How's newlywed life treating you?"

"It's fine," she replied, and then my mother turned to me. "Could we possibly chat outside?"

"Sure," I said, though I felt a sense of deeper dread wash over me. If Momma wanted to talk outside, that meant that there was a chance that she might be worried that I'd raise my voice. She'd never been a big fan of public scenes, though she hadn't backed down from a fight in her life, either. I steeled myself for what was to come.

Once we were outside, Momma said, "We need to talk

about your investigation into Evelyn's murder."

"Momma, you of all people should see how important this is. There's a cloud hanging over your new husband, and Jake might not have enough resources to find the killer without a little help from Grace and me. It's crucial that we keep digging, no matter how uncomfortable it makes things at home for you. I'm sorry that I hurt your husband's feelings, but all I'm after is the truth."

My mother looked surprised by my reaction. "Suzanne, were you under the impression that I disapproved of your involvement? To the contrary, I'm here to urge you to redouble your efforts. My husband needs your help, and rather desperately, in my opinion, but he was too stubborn to ask you himself."

"So he sent you here to talk to me?" I asked.

"Goodness no. He has no idea that I'm here." Momma hesitated a moment, and then asked me, "Have you heard about Evelyn's will?" I didn't know how to answer that, and I was still trying to come up with a reasonable answer when she added, "It appears that my husband was still the main beneficiary. What makes matters worse is that she was about to change it to her cousin."

"Julie Gray," I said, supplying the name.

"So, you know about her."

"Her name's come up, and I've even spoken with her about the situation."

Momma looked surprised by the information. "Did she know that Phillip was named in the will and not her?"

"No, I'm certain the news came as a surprise to her when Jake told her. She told me that she was getting everything Evelyn had."

"That's good news, isn't it?" Momma asked. "If she thought she was inheriting Evelyn's money, it would give her a motive for murder."

"It's on my list of possibilities," I admitted. "Are you sure you don't mind me investigating?"

"Of course not. Why should I?"

I didn't want to say it, but the words had to be spoken nonetheless. "Momma, what if I find evidence that implicates your new husband in his ex-wife's murder?"

"He didn't kill her, Suzanne. No matter what you might think of the man, he's not a murderer."

"I never thought that he was," I said quickly. "This new wrinkle looks much worse for him, though. There's something else, too."

"What's that?"

"I hate to ask you about it, but since you're here coming to me for help, I have to do it. I saw in Evelyn's appointment book that she had a meeting scheduled with Chief Martin for the day after she was murdered. Do you have any idea what that was about? Did you even know that it was going to happen at all?"

"Phillip and I don't keep secrets from each other. The meeting was my idea, as a matter of fact."

"Your idea? Why on earth would you suggest that?"

Momma shrugged. "April Springs is a small town. I shouldn't have to tell you that. Since none of us had plans of ever going anywhere else, I thought it was important to try to make peace with Evelyn. I didn't want it to be any more uncomfortable running into her at the grocery store or the gas station than it had to be."

"That's a nice thought, but it makes it appear that the chief may have had something else in mind."

"Like what?"

"Oh, off the top of my head, it could have been half a dozen things, and none of them good for you. Momma, that's my point. If I find something out about him that relates to Evelyn's murder, it's my obligation to tell Jake about it immediately. I made him that promise, and in fact, it's the only way I could get him to agree to let Grace and I investigate at all."

"By all means then, tell him. I'm confident, though, that you won't find anything else. Phillip has assured me that there are no other secrets lying in wait."

"I hope that he's right," I said. "Are we good, Momma?"

"Why do you ask such a curious thing like that?"

"I don't know. I guess I just miss you," I said. I wasn't about to remind her how unhappy she'd been with me earlier.

"Suzanne, we see each other all of the time."

"Maybe, but we're not living together anymore, and that makes a big difference in my life. Sometimes just knowing that your things are gone and that you're never coming back make me so sad."

My mother hugged me, and even though I towered over her tiny frame, I still felt small in her arms. "My dear, sweet child, you are a part of me and my life, and that's never going to change, no matter where I might live."

"I know that in my heart, but sometimes it doesn't feel that way in reality."

"Then we need to do something about that," she said with a smile as she pulled away. "I know. Let's have a few planned lunches every week, just the two of us, after you close the donut shop for the day. We can make it a special event every time that we get together."

"That sounds nice," I said.

"There was a bit of hesitation just now in your voice," Momma said. "What's wrong? Isn't that enough?"

"It's fine. I just liked it when we didn't have to plan our time together."

She caressed my cheek as she said, "Things change and life moves on, doesn't it? I miss you, too. I'm sorry if I've been so wrapped up in this new life with Phillip. I never meant to ignore you."

"You haven't," I said as I hugged her again. "I swear, sometimes I can be such a big baby. Of course you need to focus on your new marriage. I get that. Lunches do sound good, though." I frowned, and then I added, "Just not today, if that's okay. Grace and I have a few things to look into this afternoon."

"I would hope so," Momma said. "After this case is resolved, we'll institute our new plan of girl time."

"That sounds great. I love you, Momma."

"I love you, too," she said as she patted my cheek lightly. "Now, you should get back to work. It's not fair to leave Emma to fend for herself for too long."

"Are you kidding? She's enjoying it. I'll talk to you later," I said as I started back for Donut Hearts.

"Good luck, and be careful."

"Always."

Having things resolved with my mother would lighten my load considerably, and that was a good thing, since I needed to focus on catching a killer, and that took everything I had.

Chapter 18

"Hi, Grace. Give me a sec. I'm almost finished up here," I said when my best friend and fellow investigator walked into Donut Hearts two minutes after closing time. I'd sent Emma on her way a minute earlier, trying to give her a bit of a break after all of the hard work she'd done on my behalf so recently.

"No hurry here. Did I see you outside talking to your mother when I drove by earlier?"

"I didn't even notice you," I said.

"That's because I'm stealthy," she said with a grin. "Besides, you two looked as though things were getting pretty intense. Is she upset that we're investigating?"

"That's what I thought at first, but it turns out that she was asking me if we could work even harder at solving this case. I'm relieved that we're not fighting anymore."

"What made her change her mind?"

"Well, for one thing, she knows what a bind the sheriff is in, especially after Jake found out about the inheritance."

"What inheritance are you talking about?" Grace asked me.

"That's right. You haven't heard the latest development, have you? Apparently Evelyn never got around to changing her will from when she was married to the chief. Everyone, including Julie, thought that she was going to get everything, but it turns out that Chief Martin is getting it all. Not including the building Evelyn just bought with Beatrice, I'm guessing that the chief's going to get about three hundred grand, not to mention the house."

"You know what? That doesn't even surprise me," Grace said.

"Why not?" I asked her. "It shocked the daylights out of me."

"Suzanne, think about it. The woman still had her wedding picture on display long after the divorce. Clearly Evelyn had a problem with letting the chief go, no matter what she might have said in public."

"You could be right, but she was dating someone else. If she was seeing Conrad Swoop, she couldn't have still been carrying that much of a torch for Chief Martin."

"Maybe that explains the meeting she had with her attorney, and the one she'd scheduled with the chief as well."

"Momma had something to do with that one, I'm afraid," I said as I ran the reports from the cash register.

"Your mother set it up?" Grace asked incredulously.

"She wanted them to all at least get along on the surface, given how small April Springs can be sometimes."

"I didn't know the boundaries changed that frequently."

"You know what I mean," I said as I finished counting out the money in the register. "Huh. Well, that's not good."

"What's not?"

"I'm short twenty dollars," I said after I counted the money again.

"Somebody got more change back than they deserved to," Grace said lightly.

"I can't believe it happened," I said as I counted one more time, with the exact same results.

Grace reached into her purse and pulled out a bill. Slapping the twenty down on the counter, she said with a smile, "There you go. Problem solved."

I handed the bill back to her. "Thanks, but not really. I can't believe I slipped up like that." I pulled the till out of the register, and then looked below it. On rare occasions, money slipped down there, and eureka, there was the errant twenty. "Found it," I said triumphantly as I waved it overhead.

"Well, I'm just glad that we got that settled, because I

might not have been able to sleep tonight," she said with a wry grin.

"You're joking, but it would have been enough to keep me awake. It's been tough enough getting used to the work and the hours again, but I couldn't handle it if I started making simple mistakes making change. I pride myself on being competent in a world that doesn't always stress perfection."

"As for me, I like to phone it in most of the time," she said.

"I'm not kidding."

"Neither am I," Grace answered. "There's nothing all that precise about my job, especially since so much of it involves being a supervisor. My people either meet their sales goals, or they don't. Shoot, I don't even run the totals myself."

"Then how do you know the level of their performance?"

"Corporate tells me, trust me on that. When my people underachieve, I get a call from my boss. When they do something exemplary, I get an email."

"And when they're just plain average?"

"Then nobody says anything at all. That's the state of being I prefer."

"You don't want overachievers working for you?" I asked as I finished up the deposit slip and got everything ready for the bank.

"No way. If I have too many of those on my staff, then they get antsy and start gunning for my job. No ma'am, I'll take status quo every day of the week."

"I'm glad I have just the one employee."

"This place is so small, if you had any more than that, you'd have to step outside to change your mind."

I looked around the shop and smiled. "It might be cozy, but it's all mine, and I like it."

"I do, too," Grace replied. "After the bank, where should we go?"

"I don't know about you, but I'd like to ask Julie about that birthday card we found in Evelyn's trashcan. I've got a hunch that things weren't as sweet between them as she wanted me to believe the last time we chatted."

"Oh, goody. I just love an ambush, especially when it's someone else that's in your crosshairs."

"I never ambush anybody, do I?" I asked.

"Maybe that's a little too harsh of a way to phrase it, but yes, you can ask questions abruptly when we're grilling our suspects."

"Should I change the way I interview people?" I asked her, honestly concerned about the way that I came across.

"No way, Suzanne. It's really the only way that we get honest reactions most of the time. If anything, I believe that we should do it more often."

I smiled at her, and then I said, "I'm not so sure about that, but whatever we've been doing so far seems to have been working. We've had more than our share of success in the past, even if some of it has been due directly to luck."

"If by luck you mean preparation meeting opportunity, then I agree with you wholeheartedly."

"Someone famous said that, didn't they?" I asked, vaguely remembering hearing that particular quote before.

"Of course they did. I like to think that I'm famous, if nothing else, in my own mind."

"You're famous to me, too," I said. "Let's drop this deposit off, and then we can go looking for Julie."

"I'm glad we have a bit of a car ride. That way we can scheme a little more as we head to Union Square," Grace said as we locked up Donut Hearts and headed for my Jeep.

"I prefer to call it strategizing," I said, grinning slightly.

"Potato, potato," she said, with absolutely no change in inflection from the first to the second pronunciation.

"Julie, I'd love to chat, if you've got the time," I said. Fortunately, we'd found her at her apartment. Unfortunately, she was walking out the door as we'd been walking up the steps to her place.

Evelyn's cousin glanced at her watch, and then she said, "I don't have much to spare, to be honest with you. What's this about?"

"We'll make it as quick as we can. It's about our earlier conversation," I said.

"And who exactly is this?" she asked me as she pointed directly at Grace.

"This is my best friend, Grace Gauge," I said as Grace offered her hand. Julie took it as I continued, "She's helping me look into your cousin's murder."

"So, you're investigating after all. Suzanne, I don't mean to be rude, but what makes you believe that you are better qualified to solve Evelyn's murder than the police?"

"I don't, not necessarily. Think of us as supplemental assistance," I said.

"What could you possibly do that would help anyone involved in the case?"

"Lots of things," Grace said. "For instance, we know that you got shut out of another will, and that you aren't getting a dime from Evelyn's estate, either."

Julie frowned at that. "I didn't think that would be common knowledge. I'll have to have a word with the state police inspector."

"Actually, my mother told me," I said, addressing the statement myself.

Julie nodded. "And she's married to Chief Martin now. My, you have a cozy little situation going on in April Springs, don't you?"

"We like it," I said.

"I'm sure there's nothing else that you know," she said confidently.

"I wouldn't be so sure of that," Grace said.

Julie looked at her sharply. "What do you mean by that?"

I'd been holding the torn card for later, but it was out there now, so I didn't have any choice but to address it. After I explained what we'd found, I added, "It was found in Evelyn's trashcan."

My statement didn't seem to faze her in the least. "My dear cousin was never really very sentimental," she said brusquely. "That doesn't surprise me."

"I don't know that's at all true. As a matter of fact," I said, "she still had her wedding photo with the chief on display in her house."

Grace piped up, "And as for the card, it wasn't just discarded. It was torn in half, too."

Julie just shrugged at hearing the news. "Why on earth should I believe you, or even care about it if it happens to be true?"

I pulled out my phone and showed her the picture, glad that I'd thought to take it. "Here's the evidence, if you don't believe us."

Julie looked at it, and then to my surprise, she smiled.

"What's so funny?" Grace asked.

"Did either one of you actually bother reading the card?" Julie asked us.

I hadn't even thought about doing it, and evidently neither had Grace. "No," I said. "What does that have to do with how we found it?"

"My cousin and I had a running gag about birthday cards. We tried to find ones that were disrespectful, inappropriate, or in any way not acceptable. It started when I was a kid and she sent me a card for my seventh birthday congratulating me on my retirement. That part of the message was crossed out, and she'd written in that I'd retired from being her favorite cousin. Mean, but funny, too. I found a condolence card for her next birthday, marked through it, and added a message that I was sad about her being so old. My mother had a fit when she found out about it, but Evelyn had enjoyed it, so we kept the tradition up over the years."

I tapped my phone to study the message a little closer, and I was surprised to see that the card was originally intended for someone on their hundredth birthday. Sure enough, on the face of it, Julie had written, "You don't look a day over 99" on it.

Julie said, "I would have loved to see her face when she read that one. It would have been priceless."

"I'm sure that it was," I said.

As I showed the image to Grace, Julie said, "Now, if you'll excuse me, I really do have to get going. Phillip may be inheriting everything of my cousin's, but I'm still in charge of her funeral arrangements, and if I don't leave right now, I'm going to be late."

"Thanks for taking the time to chat with us," I said, but she didn't linger long enough to respond.

"That was odd," I said after she was gone and we were left standing there on her porch.

"I don't know. I thought it was kind of funny. Maybe we should start exchanging cards like that. It could be a real hoot."

"If it's all the same to you, I'd rather not," I said. "The real question is, does that make Julie look guiltier in our view, or less?"

"About the same, I'd say," Grace replied as we headed back to the Jeep. "I hate when we're stalled on a case like this. After we speak with a suspect, I'd rather we clear them or believe even more that they're guilty. Ambivalence is not going to do us any good."

"Unfortunately we both know that sometimes that's how it works," I said.

"Hopefully we'll have more luck with Violet."

"If not with her," I answered, "then perhaps with Conrad."

"For having so many suspects, we're not doing great eliminating many of them, are we?"

"Not so far, but we're not the only ones working on this, remember? Jake could be chipping away at the list even as we speak."

"Hey, as long as one of us is advancing this case, I'll be happy," Grace said. "Now, let's go see what Violet has to say for herself."

"At least she and Conrad both live in Union Square," I said as I started the Jeep. "It's nice to be able to talk to three suspects in one trip."

"There's that," Grace said. "Maybe if there's time later, we can get another bite at Napoli's."

I glanced over at her sleek form as I said, "For someone with such a slim figure, you sure do dream about Italian food an awful lot."

"What can I say? I have a strong metabolism. Sometimes it can be a real curse."

"Feel free to share some of that with me," I said. "I can just talk about Angelica's restaurant and gain three pounds."

"We each have our strengths," Grace said with a grin.

"And weaknesses, as well," I replied. "Let's go tackle Violet and see if we can discover what her shortcomings are."

Chapter 19

"Hey, Violet," I said when she finally came to her door. I'd nearly given up hope that she was going to answer, but she finally made it. From the look of things, she'd hastily gotten dressed, though it was late afternoon. Two buttons on her blouse were undone, and her hair was disheveled. Had we just woken her up? Maybe that would play in our favor if she were still a little groggy from her nap.

"What do you two want now? I thought we were finished talking."

"You might be done, but we're not," Grace said. "We would still love to hear where you were when Evelyn was murdered. You never told us the last time we spoke."

"You're not the police. I don't have to tell you a thing," she said.

"Who's at the door, Violet?" a familiar man's voice asked from the other room.

"Nobody important," she told him, and then she faced us again. "Go away. Now."

To punctuate her demand, she slammed the door in our faces.

"Did you hear that man's voice inside?" I asked Grace as we left the porch. "It was Conrad Swoop, wasn't it?"

"That's who it sounded like to me. It didn't take him long to come back to Violet, did it?"

"If he ever left her in the first place," I said.

"What do you mean?"

"Grace, what if he was *always* interested in her more than he was in Evelyn? He could have played the chief's ex-wife for a fool, swindled some money out of her, and then got rid of her so he could be with Violet. It might have been his plan all along."

"I suppose it's a possibility," Grace said a little uncertainly.

"You don't buy it?"

"I'm not sure," she answered as we got into the Jeep. "Tell you what. Why don't you drive around the block, and then park somewhere out of sight up the street?"

"What do you have in mind?"

"To be honest with you, I'd like to see where Conrad goes after he leaves here," Grace answered.

"What if he's settled in for the rest of the day?"

Grace shrugged. "Tell you what. We'll give him half an hour, and if he hasn't left her place by then, we'll go on to the next thing on our list. How does that sound to you?"

"It's a better idea than anything I've got," I said as I proceeded to do just what she'd suggested. I parked far enough down the block to see Violet's front door, but not be obvious to anyone looking out the window from inside.

After half an hour of surveillance, there was still no sign of Conrad.

"That's it," Grace said. "We can go now. Sorry my idea was a bust."

"Hey, I still think it was worth a shot. Shall we go look for Beatrice now?"

"We might as well," Grace said, and then she grabbed my hand before I could start the Jeep back up. "Hang on a second. Look over there."

I did as she suggested, but nothing was going on near Violet's front door. The movement was coming from behind her house. Slinking around the corner trying his best to look inconspicuous was none other than Conrad Swoop himself.

"Who exactly is he hiding from?" Grace whispered, even though there was no way that he could hear us from where he was at the moment.

"I don't know, but he looks pretty guilty, doesn't he? The real information I want to know is where exactly is he going now?"

We watched as Conrad went to his car, slid inside quickly, and then drove off.

"Don't follow him too closely," Grace said as I started the Jeep's engine.

I grinned at her. "Don't worry about me. After all, this isn't my first rodeo."

We followed Conrad from a distance, but in the end, it turned out to be another disappointment. After stopping at a fast-food restaurant window for takeout, he headed straight home, and from the look of things, that was where he was going to stay.

"I guess we should go see Beatrice now," I said as we watched him duck inside.

"Why not? I can't believe that this idea didn't pay off."

"You know how this goes, Grace. We run into a lot of dead ends when we investigate, and besides, we learned something valuable."

"What, that Conrad was still with Violet?"

"That, and the fact that he doesn't want anyone to know about it. Why else would he have slipped out the back door like that?"

"Maybe he was afraid that we were still watching him," she answered.

"A fear that turned out to be well founded," I said.

We found Beatrice working out in her garden when we neared her house. "At least we know that she's home," Grace said.

"Yes, but that doesn't mean that she'll be willing to talk to us any more than Violet was."

"Maybe not, but she can't exactly run away, can she?"

At that moment, I spotted something odd, so I kept driving past Beatrice's house without slowing down.

"Where are you going, Suzanne?"

"Did you see what she was doing just then?" I asked.

"All I noticed was that it was kind of odd the way she was looking around so furtively, but what does that prove?"

"Grace, I was watching her hands. She was burying something in her garden in plain sight."

"How can you be so sure of that?"

"I watched her drop something in a hole and quickly cover it back up. What on earth could that mean?"

"Are you sure she wasn't just planting something?"

I shrugged. "In the walkway and not in the bed?" I asked. "Why would she plant anything there?"

"What should we do about it?"

"I say we go somewhere and kill a little time," I said. "After that, we can come back here and dig up whatever she was just burying."

"Suzanne, how sure are you about what you just saw?"

"I'm fairly certain of it," I said.

"My question is, are you sure enough to try to explain it all away if we get caught disinterring something that's none of our business?"

"Hey, we've talked ourselves out of worse situations than that before," I said.

"That's true enough, but there might be a time when our charm doesn't work. I know, it's hard for me to believe even as I'm saying it, but still, it could happen."

"You're right. If we come back later, Beatrice might catch us, or worse yet, someone else might see what we're up to. Grace, we have to find out what she buried, and I mean right now."

"How do you propose we do that?" she asked me.

"One of us needs to distract her while the other one recovers the buried treasure."

"Which one do you want to do?"

I grinned at her. "Hey, it was my idea. I'll let you pick."

"I'll always take action over talk. You find a way to keep her occupied, and I'll do the digging."

"I was afraid that you'd choose that option," I said. I circled the block, but when we got back to Beatrice's place, she was no longer in her garden at all. "Has she gone already?"

"Let's go knock on the front door first," Grace said.

"Tell you what. I'll go to the door by myself. If she's there, we don't want her to know that you're with me. It should make sneaking into her garden and digging up whatever she's hiding a little easier."

"Good plan. I'll duck down as you walk to the door, and then I'll slip out once we know where she is. How does that sound to you?"

"It's as good a strategy as any," I said. "Wish me luck."

"Right back at you."

I walked to the front door, and as I waited for her to answer her doorbell, I tried to come up with something that might keep Beatrice from noticing Grace sneaking into her garden. I still wasn't quite sure about how to do that when she finally came to the door.

"Suzanne, what are you doing here?" Beatrice asked me as she answered her door.

It was a fair question. I just wished I had an answer for it. After a brief hesitation, I blurted out the first thing that I could think of. "I'm here about your building."

"My home?" she asked, clearly puzzled by my statement.

"No, the one in April Springs. Since you said that your plans to open a candle shop weren't going to work out, I thought you might be interested in selling the place." As I spoke, I hoped that Grace was in action, but it took all of my willpower not to look over in the direction of Beatrice's garden. Hopefully Grace was skulking her way toward it, but I wasn't about to draw Beatrice's attention to her if she was.

"Why on earth would you want to buy it?"

It was another fair question. Stalling, I said, "I've been thinking about opening a shop there myself."

"What kind of shop?"

"Soap," I said, blurting out the first thing that had come to my mind.

She looked surprised. "But I thought you were a donutmaker?"

"I am, but it wouldn't hurt to diversify. Donut Hearts is doing really well, and I thought it would be good to branch out into something else."

"I had no idea that a donut shop could do that well," she said.

Neither did I, but since I was bluffing, I might as well go all the way. "You'd be amazed by the profits I generate on a daily basis." That was probably true. She'd be amazed by just how little I actually made, but I wasn't about to clarify. "My mother has long dabbled in many different directions, so I figured it was high time I started growing my portfolio myself." Wow, I was just glad that I didn't have Pinocchio's nose at the moment. It would have been growing beyond reach with every word.

"It's a sound idea, but I'm afraid that I can't help you."

"I thought the business was yours to sell now," I said.

"It may be someday, but it will be tied up in Evelyn's estate for several months, if not years, before I get free title to it, and that depends on when they find and convict her killer. There's no way that the property is going to be released before then."

"I see," I said, trying to hide my faux disappointment. I finally risked a glance in the direction of the garden and saw Grace slipping back into my Jeep. "Well, I understand, but keep me in mind, okay?"

"I will," she said. "And thanks for stopping by."

"You're most welcome," I said.

I was three steps away from her front door, and that much closer to the Jeep, when Beatrice said in an icy voice, "Hold on. Stop right where you are."

What had just happened? Had she seen Grace digging up her treasure?

It appeared that we were busted.

"What's wrong?" I asked as I turned back to her. I kept my most innocent expression plastered on my face as I faced her.

"Something's not right," she said sternly as she looked steadily over at her garden.

"What do you mean?"

Instead of answering immediately, she passed me and started for the Jeep. I thought Grace had made a clean getaway, but when I looked at the ground, I saw that she'd tracked a bit of mud on one shoe. The trail clearly led from the garden straight to my Jeep.

I followed along, but there was nothing else that I could do to stop her, though I tried, though it was to no avail. "What's going on?"

As Beatrice pulled open the Jeep's passenger door, she said, "That's what I'd like to know." Then she spotted the small package in Grace's hands and her face drained of all color. "I can't believe that you just did that. What's wrong with you? You two need to come inside right now."

"What is this?" Grace asked as she refused to move and held the packet up. "Why shouldn't we ignore you and take this straight to the police?"

"You're welcome to do just that, but if you want to know the truth, then you'll have to come with me."

I looked at Grace and asked her, "What do you think?"

"No way I'm going anywhere with her. I think we should drive as fast as we can to the police station. How about you?"

I couldn't imagine being stupid enough to go inside with a woman who might be a killer. Then again, if she hadn't done it, didn't she have the right to explain herself before we did something too rash? That's when I made up my mind. "Beatrice, neither one of us is crazy enough to go inside with you, but if you'd like to explain what's going on out here, we'll give you the opportunity. I'm sorry, but that's the best that we're going to be able to do." I was willing to bet that Beatrice didn't have a weapon on her, and if we stayed outside in the open in front of anyone who might be looking in our direction, Grace and I would likely still be safe.

At least I hoped that was the case, but I knew as well as anyone that sometimes, desperate times called for desperate measures, and if we'd just stumbled onto something that might implicate Beatrice in Evelyn's murder, the woman before us might be more dangerous now that she'd been cornered than Grace or I could ever know.

"What do you say?" I asked her.

Beatrice seemed to think it over, and finally, she shrugged, looking as though she was on the brink of hysterical tears. "Why not? I don't see what I have to lose at this point." She looked around at her neighbors' homes and added, "Could we at least go over to my garden bench? It will be better if I don't have to look at either one of you when I tell you this."

"What do you think, Grace?"

"I don't see what it could hurt," she said, and then she turned to Beatrice. "Don't try anything, though. We'll both be watching you."

"You don't have to worry about me. I'm not going to do a thing," she said.

But could we trust a possible killer, maybe even with our lives?

In the end, there was only one way to find out.

Chapter 20

"So, what's in this packet?" Grace asked Beatrice as we walked over to her garden bench.

"If it's all the same to you, I'd rather start at the beginning and tell this in my own way," she said.

"Why not? Go on. It's your story," I said.

She took a deep breath, and then she began to talk. "Last year I met a man in Asheville, a tall, handsome, charming man who was too good to be true. To make a long story short, it turned out that's exactly what he was. I didn't find out until nine months after we'd begun to see each other that he was married, and by then I was too addicted to him to break it off, even though I knew that I should do exactly that."

"What's that got to do with Evelyn?" Grace asked.

"Be patient. I'm getting to that. As I said, I kept seeing him, breaking it off, and then starting up again. He's been like some kind of drug to me." She took in a deep breath, and then she let it out slowly before she continued. "In a moment of weakness, I confessed everything to Evelyn the day that she died."

"You mean that she was murdered," I said, correcting her. I wasn't about to let her refute the distinction.

"Murdered," Beatrice amended. "Evelyn told me that if I wanted to start a new life, a new business with her, I'd have to end it with Bryce. We fought, and I stormed out of the building. It didn't take me long to realize that she'd been right, though. I drove to Asheville, and I confronted Bryce, telling him that we were through forever. He laughed at me; he laughed as though I was nothing to him. Can you imagine how cruel that was?"

"What did you do?" I asked, forgetting for the moment about Evelyn's murder and focusing on Beatrice's pain instead.

"What could I do? I hurried back here, only to find that

Evelyn was dead. Two dreams died that day, and now I'm lost and all alone."

"I'm sorry that happened to you," Grace said, not entirely unsympathetic herself. "But what's that got to do with this?" She held the packet she'd dug up for emphasis.

"Open it if you need to," Beatrice said with calm resignation. "Inside it, you'll find a few brief notes, a couple of photographs, some receipts, and the card from the flowers the one time Bryce cared enough to send them. It's our whole relationship in there. I was going to burn it all, but then I decided to bury it instead." With that, she began to cry.

I put an arm around her as Grace slit open the packet to confirm Beatrice's story. At first I was surprised by the move, but in an instant, I knew that it had been the right thing to do. If Beatrice were lying to us, we needed to know, but if she were telling the truth, then this would give her an alibi, even though she clearly hadn't realized it yet. Grace glanced through the materials inside the packet, then nodded to me as she closed it back up.

"Beatrice, you're about to be very glad that we found this," I said as I patted her shoulder.

"I don't see how. I'm completely humiliated by what I've done."

"We all make mistakes, and as you said, you didn't know that he was married at first. That should give you at least a little absolution."

She wasn't about to accept that, though. "Would you still feel that way if it had been your husband I was seeing and not someone else's?"

That was a little too close to home. I had indeed been on the other end of that situation, and my feelings toward the woman who'd cheated with my husband hadn't eased much to the day that she'd been murdered herself. "It happened to me, and I didn't forgive her when I had the chance," I admitted.

"Could you forgive her now?" Beatrice asked me.

"Believe me, I would if I could, but she's dead now," I said. "That's no excuse, though. I did manage to forgive my ex-husband finally, but it was a long, slow, and painful process."

"There you go, then," Beatrice said.

Grace wasn't having any of it, though. "Hang on a second. You need to stop being so hard on yourself, Beatrice. You made a mistake, and you compounded it based on what you just told us, but that doesn't mean that you're condemned by it forever. Make amends if you can, forgive yourself for messing up, and then get on with your life."

"I don't see how I can do that," she said in a whisper.

"Beatrice, don't you see? This is the perfect time. You have no ties now, nothing holding you back. Move forward and get on with the rest of your life."

I wasn't sure how she was going to react, but after a few moments, she nodded and looked directly at Grace. "You're right. I've got to quit beating myself up about what I did in the past. The important thing is that I never do it again in the future."

"Are you going to be able to do that?" I asked her gently.

Beatrice smiled gently. "I'll manage, even if it kills me." She let out a long and deep breath. "Truthfully, I feel better already. I've been carrying this around with me for a very long time. They're right when they say that confession is indeed good for the soul."

"Keep that in mind when you tell Jake Bishop your story," I said as I pulled out my cellphone.

"Must I?" she asked. "I'd be so embarrassed. Couldn't you do it for me?"

"Sorry, but he's going to need to hear this directly from you. Do you have any problem with us showing him your packet?"

She waved a hand in the air. "Do what you wish with

them. They are memories that I'm finished with, once and for all."

"Jake's going to have to contact Bryce, you know," Grace said, and then she added with a wicked grin, "If you'd like, we can ask him to wait until the man's wife is at home."

Beatrice seemed to hesitate as she considered it, but finally, she shook her head. "No. That's just not right. I won't be responsible for a marriage ending. If she leaves him, I don't want it to be because of me."

"Who knows? Maybe you owe it to her to tell her what's been going on," Grace suggested.

"I think she must at least suspect something," Beatrice said. "There have been too many clues in the past to suggest otherwise. Telling her might be the right thing to do, but I can't bring myself to do it. I have a suspicion that this isn't the first time he's done it, and I'm pretty sure that it won't be the last. If she chooses to turn a blind eye to his behavior, who am I to rub her face in it?"

"That's an issue for another day," I said as I called Jake. "Right now, we need to take care of your situation."

Jake picked up on the second ring.

"Where are you right now?" I asked him.

He laughed. "Hi, Suzanne. I'm fine. And you?"

"I'm good," I said with a hint of a grin, something I knew that he'd be able to read in my voice. "If you're not busy, you might want to drive over to Union Square."

"I'm already here," Jake said. "As a matter of fact, I just left Violet's place. You're not going to believe what I found out she's been doing."

"Do you mean the fact that she's sleeping with Conrad, and she may never have stopped, even though he was dating Evelyn, too?"

Jake whistled. "Remind me never to underestimate you again."

"Thanks, but that's not why I called. You need to

come straight over to Beatrice's house. She's got something to tell you."

"Is she going to confess?" Jake asked in dead seriousness.

"No, but she can provide an alibi now."

"Then why wouldn't she give me one earlier?" Jake asked as I heard him start his car.

"She said that she was too embarrassed to tell you the truth, but now that she's had a little time to think about it, she's ready to talk to you."

"I'll see you in four minutes, then," Jake said as he hung up.

"He'll be here soon," I said as I started to stand.

Beatrice looked upset. "You two aren't going to leave me, are you?"

"We thought you might like some privacy," I said.

"I have nothing to hide now. Could you both please stay with me?" The pleading in her voice and her gaze were enough to break my heart, and I could see that Grace was reacting the same way.

"We'll stay," I said.

"There's no place else we'd rather be," Grace added, patting her hand.

And we did.

After she gave Jake the same story that she'd given us, he stood and thanked her. "I'll go confirm this right now, but if everything you've told me is the truth, you should be fine."

"I wasn't sure before, but I am now," Beatrice said.

"I was talking about the investigation," Jake said.

"I was referring to my life," she replied.

Before Jake could get away, I asked, "Do you have a second?"

"Just about that," he said.

"I'll walk you back to your car," I said.

"I'll stay here with Beatrice," Grace added.

Once we were out of their hearing range, I asked, "You

believe her, don't you?"

"I don't see any reason not to," Jake said. "All I need to do is to get confirmation that this Bryce fellow actually saw her in Asheville when Evelyn was being murdered."

"What if he lies to you? It's entirely possible, you know."

"That's a good point," Jake said as he reversed direction and rejoined Beatrice and Grace. As he reached for the packet still in Grace's hand, he asked Beatrice, "May I borrow these for a few days?"

"Take them," she said.

"You'll get them back soon, so don't worry."

"I don't want them. Throw them off a bridge, burn them in a fireplace, I don't care. I just never want to see any of that again."

"Understood," Jake said, and then we walked back to his car. "We make a good team, Suzanne. Thanks for that."

"You're most welcome. Thanks for letting us stay while you talked to Beatrice."

"We both know that I wouldn't have been able to get anything out of her without the two of you."

"Will you be back in time for dinner?"

Jake looked at his watch, and then he shook his head. "It's ninety minutes to Asheville, and then I have to track this adulterer down. When I'm finished with him, I've got another ninety minutes to drive back, so I'll probably get back long after you've gone to sleep."

"I can stay up," I said.

"And be groggy tomorrow on my account? Don't worry. We'll have some time together tomorrow. I'll make sure of it."

"That would be wonderful," I said. "Have a safe trip."

"I'll do my best," Jake said, and then he glanced toward the garden where Beatrice and Grace were discussing something quite serious from the look of it. Jake took advantage of the situation and kissed me, quickly but thoroughly. "Bye, Suzanne."

"Good-bye," I said, and I stood there until he'd driven away.

When I rejoined the women, Grace stood. She told Beatrice, "Call me when you get back from your sister's place. We'll work this out."

"Thank you both," Beatrice said as she hugged us in turn, and Grace and I left.

"What was that all about?" I asked her as we began our drive back to April Springs.

"I'm going to give Beatrice a makeover," Grace said. "What can it hurt? It might help her self-esteem a little, since it's pretty battered as it is right now."

"You're okay in my book," I told Grace. Her work for a large cosmetics company allowed her many fringe benefits, flexible working hours, and a great many free samples. I hadn't taken much advantage of those, but it appeared that Beatrice was about to.

"We're not just working on her outer beauty," Grace said. "There's a funny, sweet woman inside that shell, and I'm going to do everything in my power to bring her out into the sunlight."

"Let me know if there's anything I can do to help," I said.

"Will do. So, I'm guessing that Jake isn't going to make it back in time for dinner, is he?"

"No," I admitted. "Do you have plans with Officer Grant?"

"Stephen is working overtime as long as your boyfriend is still in charge. Jake believes that he's been underutilized in the past, and he's making up for it."

"That's got to be a real morale booster," I said.

"It is, but our social life is on the back burner until further notice."

"Welcome to the club," I said.

"Well, just because the men can't join us, there's no reason that we can't go out somewhere to eat, is there?"

"Did you have any place in particular in mind, or do I even have to guess?"

Grace looked down at her clothes. "I don't think I'm dressed nicely enough for Napoli's," she said.

"Nonsense. You look fine."

"Well, we could always eat in the kitchen with Angelica and whichever daughter is helping her out back there."

"My guess is that it's Sophia," I said. She was Angelica's youngest daughter, already showing her mother's flair in the kitchen.

"That's even better," Grace said. "Do you think we could slip in the back way?"

"I don't know why not," I said. "I'm sure that Angelica would love to have us."

"Then what are we waiting for? Let's go get something to eat."

Chapter 21

"You girls are both too skinny," Angelica said as she heaped our plates with pasta, ravioli, and salad. As we'd hoped, she'd graciously invited us into her kitchen, and had taken great pleasure in feeding us.

"They can't eat all of that," Sophia said as she studied our plates.

"Nonsense. Men like women with curves."

"I don't know what men *you're* talking about," Sophia said, "but Barry likes me just the way I am." Evidently Barry was Sophia's latest boyfriend, though there was no shortage of young men applying for the position. And why not? She was a classic Italian beauty, with dark brown hair, luminous brown eyes, and a face that wars had started over in history. In truth, all of Angelica's daughters were lovely, but none of them could hold a candle to their mother.

"Barry has good taste. I'll say that much for him," Angelica said, and then she scolded, "Sophia, keep an eye on that chicken."

"I'm watching it, I'm watching it," she protested.

"This is so fun," Grace said to me after she took her first bite. "I'm glad you suggested it."

"You can't beat the food *or* the ambience," I said with a smile. While it was true that the food was unbelievably good, that was just part of it. I loved being where the action was in the kitchen, hearing the give and take between Angelica and her daughters as they served their diners.

"So, why are you both here without the men in your lives?" Angelica asked as she paused at the small table Grace and I were sharing in one corner of the kitchen.

"That's no question to ask them," Sophia said, chiding

her mother.

"You worry about the food; I'll take care of my friends."

"They're my friends, too," Sophia corrected her.

"You keep feeding us like this and we'll be everyone's friends," I said with a smile. "To answer your question, our guys are both working on a murder case."

Angelica crossed herself as she nodded. "Evelyn Martin. Of course." She hesitated, and then asked us, "You are both working on the case yourselves, am I right?"

"We're trying to lend a hand," I said.

"You're being too modest. If it helps, I'm a good listener. Sometimes I like to talk to work things out myself. How many suspects do you have left on your list?" she asked as she stirred a pot of red sauce.

I glanced at Grace, who just shrugged. Why not? "Well, we've finally got it narrowed down to Robby Chastain, the neighbor she was in a property dispute with; Julie Gray, her cousin; Conrad Swoop, her boyfriend; and his other girlfriend, Violet Frasier."

"Violet? I knew that she was dating Conrad, but I wasn't aware that he was seeing Evelyn, too, though it doesn't surprise me one bit. That man is a cad, plain and simple."

Sophia looked up from the chicken she was watching long enough to say, "He asked Mom out last year. She turned him down, and he acted as though it broke his heart."

Angelica shook her head as she rolled her eyes. "Acted is the correct word. It was all an act, but I'm not surprised that Violet believed him, and she probably still does. She's been craving a man's affection and approval since her father walked out on his family when she was only thirteen years old."

"I didn't know that," I said as I paused eating the bite of ravioli on my fork.

Angelica's spatula bobbed up and down as she pointed it at me. "Suspects are people, too, Suzanne. It would be good to keep that in mind."

"I will," I said, and then I ate the bite. "What do you think? You're from Union Square. Could Violet, Julie, or Conrad have done it?"

"Conrad wouldn't surprise me, if he got something out of it. The man is constantly creating schemes to separate people from their money, and this wouldn't be the first time that he's gotten himself into a hole doing something that he shouldn't have been doing."

"Care to give us any details about that?" Grace asked.

"No, sadly that story is not mine to tell."

"We understand," I said. "What about Julie or Violet?"

"Julie's capable of just about anything," Sophia said.

"What are you talking about?" Angelica asked her.

"You're not the only one with sources around town and stories that you aren't at liberty to tell. Let's just say that you should be careful around her."

"We plan to," I said. "What about Violet?"

Angelica shook her head. "It just doesn't fit. Have you tried to get an alibi from her?"

I shrugged. "She won't tell us or the police where she was when Evelyn was murdered."

"Maybe I can help there," Angelica said as she put her spatula down and wiped her hands on a towel.

"Do you think she'll actually tell *you*?" Sophia asked.

"Why not?" Angelica asked. "Besides, what can it hurt to ask? I'll be right back," she added as she headed for her office just off the kitchen.

"This is delicious," I told the youngest daughter as I finished a bite of pasta. "Did you make this, or did your mother?"

Sophia beamed with pride. "Nobody can tell mine from hers. None of the other girls can say that."

"How are your sisters doing?" I asked. Maria and Antonia had been waiting tables, but we hadn't had much time to chat. Things must have really been hopping outside in the dining room.

"They're all fine. Tiana is thinking about coming back. Isn't that great? We don't have much time for our own lives with the restaurant, but we all still manage to get a little fun in every now and then."

"Speaking of fun," Grace said with a smile, "tell us about this new guy you're dating."

She gave us a quick update as her mother came out of her office, looking quite pleased with herself.

"Did she actually tell you anything?" Sophia asked.

Angelica frowned. "No, she wouldn't say where she was, but I managed to find out just the same without her help."

"That's amazing," Sophia said. "I really have to hand it to you. You know this town like you know your own kitchen."

"Thank you," Angelica said proudly.

"So, where was she?" I asked her.

"In her own twisted way, I can understand why Violet wouldn't want anyone to know. It turns out that she was with Digger Jones at the time that Evelyn was murdered."

Sophia made a face. "Digger? Really? That's just gross."

Angelica looked at us as she explained, "Digger has some hygiene problems."

"That's like saying that the Grand Canyon is a little hole in the ground," Sophia said.

"The chicken needs you," Angelica reminded her daughter.

"I think it's long past needing anyone or anything," Sophia said.

"Hang on a second," I said. "Are you telling me that Violet would rather be considered a murder suspect than for folks to know that she was with this Digger guy?"

"She's clearly trying to protect her relationship with Conrad," Angelica said.

"Then she's got an odd way of going about it," Grace said.

"She was angry with Conrad for dating Evelyn, too. This was her plan to get revenge. Only with Evelyn out of the picture, Violet would rather go to jail than tell him the truth now."

"I'll have to tell Jake about this. Is that okay with you?" I asked Angelica. "He needs to know."

She thought about it, and then she shrugged. "I understand, but I can't tell you who told me about Violet and Digger."

"I bet Digger has been telling everybody he sees," Sophia said, but she still kept her gaze on the chicken, poking it lightly with the back of her tongs before turning it over in the pan for the other side to sear.

"I don't care how you found out, as long as Jake hears about this. Will you excuse me for one second?"

Angelica looked surprised. "Are you going to tell him right now?"

"Haven't you heard? We're cooperating with law enforcement these days," Grace said with a smile before she took another bite of pasta.

"Because it's Jake," Angelica said. "I don't blame you. I wouldn't be able to say no to him, either."

"He's going to love hearing that you said that," Grace said with a grin.

"He might, but we're not going to tell him, are we, Grace?" Angelica asked sweetly.

Grace got the message instantly. "No, ma'am. He won't hear a word out of me."

Angelica patted my best friend's shoulder. "That's a good girl. How's your ravioli? Would you like some more?" Before waiting for an answer, the restaurant owner scooped more out of the serving tray and replenished both our plates. I was quickly becoming stuffed, but I wasn't about to say no.

I stepped out back and called Jake. After I brought him

up to speed, he said, "I'll check it out on the way back. That's good work, Suzanne."

"It was really just Angelica," I said.

"Maybe so, but you knew where to go." He paused, and then he asked, "You're eating, too, aren't you?"

"What are you, psychic?"

That made him laugh. "Hardly. If I were you, I'd be doing the same thing. I'm afraid that there's no way that I'll see you tonight."

"I know," I said. "We'll find a way to catch up tomorrow."

"Have a good night's sleep," Jake said. "I love you. You know that, don't you?"

"I love you, too," I said, and then I hung up. It was the best way I knew how to end a conversation with him, and it always left me feeling all warm and fuzzy inside.

Back inside, Angelica pointed to me and said, "Sophia, that's the look I want you to have someday."

"You've got to be kidding," I said. "Sophia, don't change a thing. You're beautiful just the way you are right now, and I know a dozen men who would be glad to verify that fact."

She started to grin, but Angelica scolded me. "None of my daughters need any more reasons to be conceited about how pretty they may or may not be. I was talking about that smile you had. It's the look of a woman in love."

"I can't deny it," I said as I sat back at my place.

"And why would you? It's a wonderful way to feel."

"I've been in love before," Sophia protested.

Angelica just shrugged. "Maybe with boys, but that's the way a woman looks when she's in love with a man."

I chuckled softly. "This is all so delicious, Angelica. Thank you."

"Having you with us is thanks enough," she said.

After Grace and I both ate until we could eat no more,

we left Napoli's kitchen, but not before taking two massive containers filled with food with us.

"This is too much," I said to Grace once we were outside.

"Speak for yourself. I think it's perfect. I'm going to invite Stephen over for a snack when we get back to April Springs. Are you going to share yours with Jake?"

"He's welcome to all of it, but I'm afraid I won't see him until tomorrow." I was a little sad about that fact, but it would pass. After all, he'd be back at the cottage that night even if I wasn't around to greet him, and that was more than I could say when he was working on cases in the far reaches of our state.

As I drove back home, I asked Grace, "So, we have three people left on our list of suspects. Should we share our thoughts while we're driving about Conrad, Julie, and Robby?"

"It's as good a way to pass the time as any," Grace said.

"Okay, let's tackle Conrad first. He had two reasons to want Evelyn dead, the loan and his love life. If he really was with Violet all along, he might have wanted Evelyn out of the way if things were getting serious with Violet."

"Can you imagine choosing her over Evelyn?" Grace asked. "She's a bit of an obsessed stalker psycho type, isn't she?"

"Who knows? Maybe that's what Conrad likes."

"My mother always said that there was a lid for every pot," Grace said. "We never got an alibi out of him, did we? Do you think Jake's had any better luck?"

"If he has, he hasn't told me about it. What about Julie?"

"If she'd been set to inherit everything of Evelyn's, I would have an easier time believing that she could have killed her."

"True, but she didn't know that she wasn't in the will

yet, did she? If she acted on the assumption that she was set to inherit everything, it might have spurred her to action."

"Maybe," Grace said. "What about Robby?"

"At least he had an alibi, even if it was one that can't be substantiated. Working alone in his garage isn't exactly hanging out in a crowd, is it?"

"No, but you know how I feel about alibis. Only guilty people seem to have them."

"Do you honestly think Robby killed Evelyn over a tree?" I asked.

"I don't feel like we should focus on the tree. It could have easily just been the last straw in a fight between them that could have been brewing for years."

"I suppose," I said. "If you had to rank them right now, what order of likelihood would you put our suspects in?"

"As far as I'm concerned, they're all in a dead heat. Then again, if we hadn't heard Violet's alibi, I'd have been convinced that she did it, too. I hope Jake can find this Digger fellow."

"You don't believe her story?"

"I don't think Angelica lied to us," Grace said, "but her source could have been lying to her."

"Jake will check it out, I'm sure."

We were finally in April Springs, and as I passed the donut shop, I looked fondly over at the old railway depot that was now such a big part of my life. There were so many stars that had aligned perfectly to make it all possible, and buying the place had changed my life forever. I'd been in the pits of despair after Max had cheated on me, and in a rush, I'd moved in with Momma and started my own business. Both decisions had been some of the best ones I'd ever made. The donut shop had given me back my independence and self-esteem, while moving back to the cottage where I'd grown up had allowed me to reconnect with my mother in a way that I never would have done otherwise.

We were at Grace's place soon enough, and as I stopped the Jeep, I saw that Officer Grant was already on the front porch waiting for her. "We're still on for tomorrow after I close the shop, right?" I asked her as she got out and retrieved her takeout from Napoli's.

"Yes, but I might be a little late. I've got to do some spot-checking on one of my sales reps. It appears that she's been shirking her duties lately."

"Unlike you, working half days," I said with a grin.

"Hey, I'm salaried. I was told specifically by my boss that I didn't have a set schedule."

"I wonder if she meant it the way you've taken it?" I asked with a smile. "Not that I'm complaining. I couldn't do this without you."

"Well, you probably could, but it wouldn't be nearly as much fun," she said as she closed my door. "Good night."

"Night. Have a good evening."

"Oh, I plan on it," Grace said.

I waved at Officer Grant as I started to drive off, who waved back at me with a grin.

It had been nice that Grace had someone waiting for her.

The cottage was dark when I got home, and as I went inside, I flipped on enough lights downstairs to delight the power company. After stowing all of the food I'd taken from Napoli's, I sat down and wrote Jake a note before I headed upstairs to read.

Hey, Jake.

Sorry I missed you. Hope your trip was productive.

There's food in the fridge from Napoli's, and you're welcome to whatever you find there.

Wake me if you want to chat. If you don't, though, I'll see you sometime tomorrow.

Boy, this crime-fighting really gets in the way of our together time, doesn't it?

Let's hope that one of us catches the bad guy soon!

All my love,
Suzanne

I propped it up near the front door so he'd be sure to see it, and then I turned off the lights and made my way upstairs. After a quick shower, I changed into my pajamas and curled up in bed with a good book, the latest from my book club. Jennifer had called me a few days before, and we'd scheduled another meeting for the following week. I had ten days to get through this month's edition, and it was big enough to double as a doorstop. If I was going to contribute anything to the conversation, I'd better at least crack the book.

I must have fallen asleep during the prologue, because when I woke up later to my alarm, the book was still open across my stomach. As I pushed it aside, I realized that I'd have to tackle it sometime when I wasn't so tired from work and detecting.

I just wasn't sure when that might be.

Chapter 22

After I got ready for work, I tiptoed down the stairs, only to find a light on in the kitchen. Had I left it on, or had Jake? When I walked in, I was surprised to find him sitting at the table, an empty plate pushed off to one side and a stack of folders spread out across the tabletop.

"Good morning," I said as I kissed him lightly. "You didn't have to get up for me."

"I haven't been to sleep yet," Jake admitted as he stretched a little. "Thanks for leaving me dinner."

"Did you get enough to eat?" I asked as I poured myself a cup of coffee and grabbed a chair. I didn't have a lot of time to linger, but I did have a little, and I planned on taking full advantage of it.

"Plenty. I can't imagine your dinner, if those were just the leftovers."

"Don't ask," I said. "I hope your trip was at least productive."

"Very," he said as he pushed a folder away.

"Care to bring me up to date? I did give you a lead or two, after all."

Jake frowned, and then he shrugged. "Why not? For starters, Beatrice's alibi checks out."

"You actually talked to that married weasel? I hope it was in front of his wife."

"No, he was alone. Evidently she decided to leave him when she found out about the way he'd been behaving."

"Good for her," I said.

"The funny thing is, he kept asking me if I thought he could get Beatrice back."

"What did you tell him?"

"That I was a state police investigator, not Dear Abby," Jake said. "Anyway, she's off our list, and so is Violet."

"Does that mean that you found Digger?"

Jake nodded, and then he shook his head. "That man could use some tips on personal hygiene. He was more than happy to confirm that he'd been with Violet during the time of the murder. He kept trying to give me graphic details about their encounter, but I finally managed to shut him up."

"So, then there were three."

"Two, actually. Hadn't you heard?"

"No, I don't have a clue as to what you're talking about."

Jake scuffled through the folders and pulled one out. "Officer Stephen Grant, taking initiative after his regular shift, decided to canvass all property owners facing Robby's garage. One woman, a Mrs. Edna Peacock, was birdwatching all morning and happened to spot Robby working in his garage through an open doorway at the time of the murder. Can you imagine having a last name like Peacock and being a birdwatcher, too? What are the odds?"

"I imagine she might have taken up the hobby *because* of her name," I said. I knew Edna slightly, and to say that she was a little off was understating things. For one example, she'd taken the Peacock moniker all too literally. Not only did she have an abundance of peacock figurines spread throughout her home, but she favored wearing clothes featuring images of the bird itself. I'd asked her once where she'd found them, and she had boasted that she'd made them all herself.

"Should I believe her?" Jake asked.

"If Edna said it, then it's true. I've never had reason to doubt her word, nor have I ever heard anyone say a cross word about her."

"So, now we have two viable suspects left," Jake said. "That's what I've been doing with these folders. I keep staring at the information, but I'm still not certain what I'm looking for. In my gut, I believe that Conrad Swoop did it, especially after what I just found out about him."

"What's that?" I asked.

Jake took a sip of his own coffee, and then he said, "We're dancing that fine line again, Suzanne. I uncovered something during a background check that isn't public knowledge."

"Don't tell me, then," I said with a smile. "It's fine."

My refusal just seemed to confuse him. "That's it? You're giving up that easily?"

"What can I say? I know when I'm on precarious ground."

Jake nodded. "Thanks for that. Tell you what. Can you hang around for one second? I need to get something out of the bedroom."

I glanced at the wall clock. I was pushing things as it was, but that was okay. So what if I had to rush a little when I got to Donut Hearts? "Sure, I can spare a minute or two."

Jake nodded, and then he tapped a folder three times before he left the room. As he'd touched it, he made eye contact, and I knew that whatever was in there was what he'd been talking about.

The moment he was gone, I opened the folder and found a police report.

Conrad Swoop had been arrested for assault three years earlier. It had taken Jake some time to dig it up because Conrad had given the cops an alias at first, and it had muddied the trail.

So, one of our suspects had a police record *and* a history of violence.

It was as big a red flag as I could imagine.

Jake coughed just outside the door, and I closed the folder and looked away.

"Sorry about that," he said when he walked back into the room.

"What did you get out of the bedroom?" I asked him with a grin.

He laughed, knowing that I was just teasing him. "To

be honest with you, I forgot what I was going in after."

"Don't worry about it. That happens to me all of the time. So, what are you going to do? It seems pretty obvious, doesn't it?"

"That's what troubles me. It's almost too easy. There's got to be something that I'm missing." He brought out another paper and handed it to me. "Look, Julie is in debt up to her eyebrows. If she was counting on getting that money from Evelyn's estate, it could have driven her to murder. When I look at the evidence one way, I think Conrad must have done it, but when I examine it from another angle, I'm sure that Julie is just as likely guilty."

"Jake, this isn't one of your normal cases. Things don't have to be overly complicated. If you have a gut feeling about it, then that's what you should act on."

"Do you and Grace have any theories?" he asked me.

"We think it's a coin toss at this point," I admitted.

"Do you still feel that way after what I just told you?" he asked as his gaze darted to the folder holding the police report of Conrad's arrest.

"I'm just as confused as you are," I admitted. I glanced at the clock again and saw that I was truly late now. "I'd love to stay and chat, but there are donuts that need to be made."

"Go. I'm glad that my insomnia at least gave me a chance to see you."

"Right back at you," I said. I gave him a quick kiss, and then I headed out into the darkness. It looked as though Conrad Swoop was most likely our bad guy. After all, he had two motives, and an arrest record to boot.

At least it would all soon be over, and my life could get back to normal, whatever that entailed these days. That meant that Jake would go back to his old job, and I would be left alone in the cottage.

Maybe I shouldn't be in such a hurry for it all to end

after all.

"That day just flew by," Emma said as we locked the front door of the donut shop a little after eleven.

"Really? I thought it dragged by, myself," I said.

"Maybe it's because you're in charge again, but I just love coming to work these days. No worries, no responsibilities, and most of the pay."

"It's not a gold mine, is it?" I asked her. "How do things look in back?"

"I'm ready on my end. You do the reports, and I'll finish up out here. We'll be out in record time. Is Grace coming by?"

"No, I got a text message from her half an hour ago. She got hung up in West Jefferson, so I won't see her until later."

"Does that mean that you need a sleuthing buddy?" Emma asked with a smile. "You know that I'm always ready to step in if I'm needed."

"Thanks. I appreciate the offer, but it's not necessary."

"So, are things winding down in the investigation?" Emma asked.

"That depends. Is my assistant asking, or the newspaper owner's daughter?"

"Point taken. I withdraw the question," Emma said, and then she smiled to show that there were no hard feelings.

As she finished sweeping the floor and wiping down the tables, I worked on the report. Counting the money, I held my breath as I compared totals, but we were perfect for the day. That gave me more satisfaction than it probably should have, but I didn't care.

There were two-dozen donuts left, and as I finished filling out the deposit slip, Emma asked me, "Do you have any use for these today?"

"I was just going to drop them off at the church, but I've got a feeling they could use a break." Oftentimes we gave our extras away to help feed those who couldn't afford our treats otherwise, but every now and then I got the distinct impression that my offerings could be a little too much sometimes. "If you'd like them, they're all yours."

"Thanks, I just might," she said. "It's not what you think."

I grinned at her. "What do I think?"

"That I'm giving them to some random guy."

"I wasn't thinking that at all."

"Really?" she asked.

"Really. If he's good enough for our donuts, then he's bound to be anything but random. Is this someone new that you're seeing?" Emma liked to change young men like some women changed shoes, early and often.

She just shrugged, but I recognized that smile.

"Tell him I said hello," I said.

Her smile brightened even more. "I'm sure I don't know what you're talking about."

"I'm sure," I said as I looked around. "If everything in the kitchen is as clean as it is out here, you can go ahead and take off."

"Thanks."

Once she was gone, I took one last look around, turned off the lights, grabbed the deposit, and headed out myself. I missed having Grace there, but I knew that her job didn't allow her to take off at will, no matter how it felt sometimes. That didn't necessarily mean that I was going to get into trouble on my own, though. Things were squarely in Jake's hands now, and as far as I was concerned, most of my work was done. We were all fairly confident that Conrad was the killer, but even if Julie had done it, he'd catch her soon enough.

I was in line at the bank to make my deposit when something occurred to me. While Grace and I had been searching Evelyn's house, we'd been interrupted before we'd had a chance to look very thoroughly. One thing in particular intrigued me. What if there was proof that Conrad had borrowed that money from Evelyn hidden somewhere inside? He'd been denying it all along, but that didn't mean that it hadn't happened. If there was a note in Evelyn's journal, or even on a memo pad somewhere in that house, it would go a long way toward helping Jake make sure that Conrad was arrested for Evelyn's murder. It might be a long shot, but what did I have to lose? Grace was out of town, and Jake was hard at work, so why shouldn't I take a chance and see if there was anything else at Evelyn's place that might tie Conrad to her murder? I made the deposit, and then I drove to Evelyn's house. I still didn't want to be seen going inside, so I parked down the block and walked back through the rear yards. The key was where we'd left it, so after going inside, I quickly punched the security code from my last visit.

I just hoped that no one had changed it. If they had, I was in for a shock.

The alarm turned itself off on my first attempt, and I breathed a sigh of relief, knowing that I was safe.

At least that's what I thought at the moment I stepped inside, no matter how wrong I turned out to be a few seconds later.

That's when I realized that I wasn't alone.

Chapter 23

In my defense, I tried to sneak back out. The last thing I wanted was a confrontation with someone who was most likely a killer.

But I couldn't quite manage it.

My hand was on the doorknob when I heard a voice behind me say, "I don't know how you figured out that it was me, but you're not going to live long enough to tell anyone else."

Chapter 24

I turned around to find Conrad Swoop staring at me. There was a wickedly big knife in his hand, one that I would be defenseless against if I tried to fight him. I would have fled if I could have, but that wasn't an option, since I'd locked the door behind me when I'd walked in.

"Conrad, I don't know what you're talking about," I said, trying to act as confused as I could. "I was here earlier and I dropped my favorite scarf. Have you seen it anywhere?"

"Nice try," he said as he neared me. I looked wildly around for something to defend myself with, but there was nothing that I could use as a weapon, especially against the knife he was threatening me with. "Step over here away from the door, Suzanne."

"If I do, then you're going to promise not to hurt me, right?"

The smile on his face chilled the blood in my veins. "I wasn't going to say that. I hate to break it to you, but this is the end for you."

"Why are you even here, Conrad?" As I looked around the house, I saw that he'd wrecked the place, obviously searching for something. "Did you lose something?"

"An IOU I wrote to Evelyn," he said in disgust. "She told me that she hid it somewhere in the house, but I can't find it anywhere."

"Is that why you killed her? Was it for the money you owed her?"

"I wanted more than that," Conrad said as he gestured with the knife. I had no choice but to follow his directions. Maybe if I could stall him long enough, someone would come save me. How I regretted not telling anyone where I was going, and that I hadn't waited for Grace to come back. Then again, if only one of us had to die, I was okay with it being me. Our investigations were motivated more by my desire to find the truth than Grace's, so it was fitting that I was the one who'd pay the ultimate price.

But not if I could help it.

I spotted a lamp turned over near where Conrad was leading me, so maybe, if I got lucky with a last-chance desperation grab, I could retrieve it and use it against him. I'd have to play things just right before I could try that, though.

"What else could you get out of her?" I asked as I edged closer and closer to the only potential weapon within reach.

"I wanted it all, so I asked the stupid woman to marry me," Conrad said, his face filling with rage for a moment. "When she turned me down, she signed her own death warrant."

"That must have stung," I said, trying to show a little false sympathy. If I could catch him off guard, so much the better.

"Don't patronize me, Suzanne. It's clear that you followed me here. How long have you been on to me? There's no use lying; I'll get the truth out of you one way or the other."

"The reality is that you made my final list, but I still wasn't convinced that it was you."

That seemed to spark a little interest in him. With a wicked grin, he asked, "Is that so? Who else made the cut?"

"Julie Gray," I said, inching just a little closer now. In another minute, I'd have my chance, and it would be over, one way or the other.

Conrad laughed. "Nice, the spurned cousin. I really should try to set her up for the fall once I've taken care of you." He looked through the open windows as he added, "Where's that little snoop buddy of yours?"

"She had to work today," I said.

"Then it turns out that this is her lucky day. How about your boyfriend?"

I pointed to the window behind him. "He's right there!"

Conrad took the bait and whirled around.

As he did, I reached down and grabbed the lamp. When I had it in my hands, I ran toward the killer, hoping to knock his head off with it.

I might have managed it, too, but he moved to one side at the last second. The blow hit his shoulder and staggered him for a moment, but he still managed to hold onto the knife.

"Stupid fool," he said as he pushed me with his free hand. At least he hadn't stabbed me. I tripped over a few books on the floor, and he stood over me, waving the knife like a baton. "I saw your reflection in the window. You wanted to use the lamp against me. Now I'm going to use it against you. Roll over onto your back and hold your hands together where I can see them."

I did as I was told, hoping for one last opening, but it never came. Conrad put a knee in my back, driving the air from my lungs for a moment. I felt his full weight on me as he jerked the lamp cord free from its base and wrapped my hands tightly with it.

I couldn't free myself from my bonds no matter how hard I struggled.

Conrad must have reached down and picked me up, because I felt myself being pulled upward, and then shoved toward one wall.

The wall where there was a closet.

Was he going to just lock me in and then make his escape?

Maybe I'd live through this after all.

The coats were all missing, with wire hangers strewn all over the floor of the small closet. He shoved me inside, and then I heard the door lock.

"Thank you for not killing me," I said in tears through the door.

"Who said anything about sparing your life?" Conrad asked, with a hint of wicked laughter coming from the other side.

"But I'm in here and you're out there," I said.

"That's right where you need to be. Now shut up. I've got something to do."

I reached down for a hanger, but I couldn't pick one up without falling down, and if I did that, I wasn't at all certain that I'd be able to get back up again. On the fourth try, I managed to snag one, but I still wasn't sure what I could do with it. Perhaps I could twist it in my tied hands and use it to free myself from my bindings? If that failed, I might be able to use it as a weapon, jabbing at his eyes if he ever opened the closet door again.

I was still working the metal back and forth in an attempt to get it to break when I smelled something, and I realized just what Conrad's plan was going to be.

"Let me out!" I shouted through the door.

A voice from just on the other side of the door said, "Smell that, do you? What's wrong, Suzanne? You run a donut shop. Surely you aren't afraid of a little fire."

The smoke was coming in under the door now. Was it getting hotter inside? "I won't tell anyone about you. I swear it."

"Sorry, but I don't believe you. I may not be able to find that IOU, but nobody else is going to, either. You'll both burn up together. Good-bye."

I was getting desperate when I heard the front door slam.

How long would I live, trapped in this upright coffin?

Would the flames get me first, or the smoke?

I'd read that the best thing to do in a fire was to go as low as possible, so I eased myself down onto the floor. But I still wasn't ready to die, no matter how it might come.

Bracing my back and my bound hands behind me, I started pushing the door with my feet. Thankfully, it wasn't a walk-in closet, but a fairly narrow affair.

Pushing didn't work.

It was time to kick.

Why had I worn tennis shoes today instead of my old hiking boots?

I kicked out, again and again, with all my strength, as the smoke continued to creep into my little jail cell. It was hopeless. The house was old and solidly built, and the door was thick wood, not a cheap modern variety.

Coughing, I drew my legs back again, and I kicked outward with everything I had.

I was rewarded with the splintering sound of the doorframe as it broke.

But was I really any better off than I had been?

The living room was ablaze, and as the flames crept up the far wall, I could feel the heat on my face as the smoke intensified.

I wasn't going to die like this if I could help it.

I inched my way across the floor and into the kitchen, where the flames were just beginning to touch. The air was heavy with the smell of gasoline, and I knew that it would be seconds before I had any chance of escaping at all.

Bracing against the kitchen window, just opposite the same place that Grace and I had spied on Chief Martin not that long ago, I worked myself up to a standing position.

How was I going to get out, though?

With my hands still firmly tied behind me, I reached down and managed to pick up a barstool.

The problem was that I couldn't do anything with it.

I tried shoving it against the window, but I couldn't break the glass, no matter how hard I tried.

The smoke was getting thicker now, the flames hotter.

There was one, last-chance act of desperation left. Against all good judgment, I moved quickly *toward* the smoke and flames instead of away from them, holding my breath the entire time.

Then, with every last ounce of strength I had left, I ran backward as hard as I could, holding the stool like a battering ram.

It felt like forever, but finally, I heard the glass crash as I fell backward into the bush I'd hidden behind, and I could smell sweet, glorious, fresh air again.

I wasn't sure how long I lay there, but the next thing I knew, Jake was kneeling beside me, freeing my arms and taking me up in his.

And that was when I blacked out again, from the stress, the relief, and the wonder, that somehow, I'd managed to escape with my life.

Unfortunately, so had Conrad Swoop.

Chapter 25

When I woke up, Jake was holding my hand. I was in the hospital, and there was an oxygen tube in my nose.

"Jake, Conrad Swoop killed Evelyn!" I tried to lift myself up in bed as I warned him, but he put a hand on my shoulder and I slipped back down.

"Take it easy, Suzanne. I got him."

"I thought he escaped," I said.

"He almost did. I've been chasing him all day, and I finally caught him trying to leave town. I'm afraid I owe the city of April Springs one police cruiser. I had to wreck him before he'd stop."

"I'm sure they'll forgive you for doing it," I said, and then I coughed a little. "Jake, can I have some water?"

He held a cup up to my lips, and I took a small sip. It felt wonderful.

"How did you find me?" I asked. "I can't believe you came to my rescue."

"No way am I taking credit for that," Jake said with a smile. "You came to your own rescue. I had to cut the cord off your wrists myself. How did you manage to throw that chair through the window and escape?"

"I didn't exactly throw it," I said.

"Then what did you do?"

"I picked it up and ran at the window with it."

"Backwards?" he asked incredulously.

"You never know what you can do until you have to," I said.

Jake stroked a stray strand of hair out of my face as he leaned forward and whispered, "I can't believe that I almost lost you."

"I wasn't about to let Conrad kill me if I could help it. How did you know to come looking for me when you did?"

"As I cuffed him, Conrad said that at least he got some satisfaction out of getting rid of you. He wouldn't say another word, even when I pushed him harder than I probably should have, but as I got close to him I smelled gasoline. I looked at the skyline and followed the smoke from there."

"You just left him in the back of your car?"

"I wrecked mine, remember?" he asked with a grin. "Actually, he was in Grant's vehicle. Officer Grant is a good man, I'll tell you that. If he hadn't been there to pull me off Conrad, I'm not sure what I would have done."

"You wouldn't have hurt him," I said, confident that Jake's better nature would have kicked in.

"Don't kid yourself. When I thought about what he might have done to you, all bets were off."

"We're both okay now, so that's really all that matters."

He kissed my forehead lightly as Momma and Chief Martin came bursting in.

"I just heard," my mother said as she rushed to the free side of my bed. "Suzanne, are you okay?"

"I'm a little bruised, and my throat's sore, but all in all, I'm just dandy," I said.

"You won't rest until you scare me to death, will you?" she asked with a smile as a tear ran down her cheek.

"Momma, I swear, I was trying to stay out of trouble, but it managed to find me, anyway."

She laughed at that. "That's my baby girl."

"I haven't been a baby in a pretty long time," I said in a raspy voice.

"In my eyes, you'll always be my baby," she said. Then Momma turned to Jake. "Thank you."

"For what? I hope nobody thinks that your daughter needed saving, because she managed to do it all on her own without any help from me, or anyone else, for that matter."

"I wasn't talking about that. I heard you caught Evelyn's killer."

Jake shrugged. "It was a team effort."

The sheriff stepped forward and shook Jake's hand. "I can't tell you how much we appreciate it."

"My pleasure. Chief Martin, we need to talk about one of your men."

The chief's face fell. "Why, did one of them mess up?"

"On the contrary. Why do you have Officer Grant riding a desk so much? He's a fine man, and an excellent law enforcement officer."

"I know that," the chief said, "and if anyone tells him I said this, I'll deny it, but I hope that he'll take my place one day."

"Perhaps one day soon," Momma said.

"Is there something that I should know about?" I asked her.

"No, we're just talking," Momma said.

"Nothing but idle chatter," the chief added, echoing her sentiment. "Are you okay, Suzanne? What you did today was a brave thing."

"Thanks, but how brave is self-preservation? I did what I had to do to survive."

"Well, not everyone would be as strong as you were," he said. "I'm proud of you."

"Thanks," I said, and then I saw Momma crying again. "If you all don't mind, I'm pretty worn out. Can we do this later?"

"Of course," Momma said. "Phillip, let's go get some of that abysmal hospital coffee they serve here."

"I'll go, too," Jake said.

"Can you hang back for a second?" I asked him.

"I'll do whatever you want me to do," he said.

After Momma and the chief were gone, I said, "I'm glad you caught Conrad."

"He's where he belongs now," Jake answered. "When I think about what he almost did to you—"

"Don't focus on that. The only thing I'm sorry about is that you have to go back to work. I'm going to miss you."

"You won't have time to, at least not right away," he said with a grin. "I put in for two weeks' vacation so I can take care of you for a change."

"Oh, I'll bet your boss just loved that. How loudly did he say no?"

"He wasn't happy about it, but he ended up giving in," Jake said.

"What did you do, threaten to quit again?"

"Hey, if it keeps working, why change strategies?"

"One of these days he's going to call your bluff. You know that, don't you?" I asked him.

"When he does, he may just find out that I wasn't bluffing after all."

What did he mean by that? "Jake, what are you thinking right now?"

He stroked my hair again, something I loved to have him do, as he said, "Suzanne, I lost someone, two someones actually, that meant the heaven and earth to me, once in my life, and I'm not about to let it happen again."

"I love you, Jake, but you can't live the rest of your life worrying about my safety. You know that, don't you?"

"Tell you what," Jake said with a smile as he stood up. "Why don't we save this conversation for when you're feeling better? Right now, all you need to do is focus on getting better."

"That I can do," I said, and then I groaned a little.

"Are you in pain?" Jake asked, suddenly alarmed.

"No, not any more than I was before, anyway. I just realized that I won't be able to open the donut shop tomorrow."

Jake laughed, a sound I was nearly certain not that long ago that I'd never hear again. It sounded better to me than a string quartet. "Emma has already been by. She and her mother are going to run Donut Hearts until you can get back to work."

"Then I know that it's in good hands," I said as I settled back down in the bed.

After Jake was gone, I had a little time to reflect on what had happened. Conrad Swoop had tried his best to end my life, but I'd fought him, and I'd won. But more importantly, my brush with death had reminded me to focus on what was important in my life: my family, my friends, and most of all, Jake.

I wasn't all that excited about being on the sidelines again as I recovered from the fire, but at least I'd have him with me, and that was a win any day of the week.

RECIPES

COW, SPOTS, AND MOOSE DONUTS

This recipe, and the one that follows just below, are for the many fans of Emily Hargraves and her beloved stuffed animals, who are alive to everyone who truly sees them. Cow, Spots, and Moose are, in real life, three stuffed friends my daughter had when she was growing up, and though she has since graduated college and moved out on her own, Spots is still with her to this day. Don't feel bad for Cow or Moose, though. Spots always travels home with my daughter when she visits, so there are reunions all of the time. In our circle, if you don't buy into the fact that the three of them are alive, you don't get very far with any of us. I could go on and on about them, but they are already quite pleased with themselves for making it into this series in the first place, and anything more would be just too much.
So, why is this recipe called Cow, Spots, and Moose Donuts? That's easy. Like the cows, they are white with black spots, or is it black with white spots? The story changes every time they tell it, so I was forced to do two recipes for this book. This one features a white donut mix with semi-sweet chocolate chips mixed into the dough.
I hope you enjoy them as much as the guys seem to!

INGREDIENTS

DRY
4 cups bread flour
1 cup granulated sugar
1/2 cup semi-sweet chocolate chips
1 1/2 teaspoons baking soda
1 teaspoon nutmeg

1 teaspoon cinnamon
2 dashes of salt

WET
1 egg, beaten
1 cup buttermilk
1/3 cup sour cream

For the glaze:
1/2 cup semi-sweet chocolate
1/2 cup heavy cream

For the white spots:
White icing

For the antlers:
Broken mini-pretzels

Oil for Frying
Canola or peanut, about 6 cups

DIRECTIONS

In a large mixing bowl, thoroughly combine the flour,
sugar, chocolate chips, baking soda, nutmeg, cinnamon,
and salt. Add the beaten egg to the mix, and then add the
buttermilk and the sour cream and stir it all in until it's
combined nicely. The amounts of buttermilk or flour
might vary slightly, but keep adding one or the other until
you can easily work with the dough. If you've ever made
homemade bread before, that's the consistency that
you're shooting for. After you've kneaded the mixture,
roll it out to about 1/4 to 1/3 of an inch thick. Use a
donut cutter to cut them out, setting aside the holes for
later. If you don't have a cutter, improvise with different

sized glasses. You should have a good idea of what a donut looks like, so be creative!

Bring your oil up to 375 degrees F, then carefully add the dough rounds. Don't overcrowd the pot, or the oil will cool too much for a clean fry.

These donuts cook for two to three minutes on each side. After one side is done, flip them so the other side has a chance to cook as well.

Let the donuts and holes cool on a rack with a paper towel underneath to catch any excess oil. While they are cooling, make the chocolate glaze using equal parts semi-sweet chocolate chips and heavy cream over a double-boiler or in the microwave. Don't overheat the mix, or the glaze will be ruined. Next, glaze the top of the donuts with the chocolate. If you're feeling especially creative, add little random irregular white icing dots, and for a taste of moose, bury a few broken mini-pretzels into one edge for the antlers!

Makes 8-10 donuts.

REVERSE COW SPOTS MOOSE DONUTS

This donut is the reverse of the one above, using different ingredients and having a totally different appearance, texture, and taste. These donuts are heavy and dense, but a real chocolaty treat. This version uses a chocolate donut recipe and adds white-chocolate chips. For the outside, use a vanilla glaze or white store-bought icing to make them spotted! Moose's antlers stay the same, using broken pretzel bits.

INGREDIENTS

WET
1 egg, beaten
2/3 cup granulated sugar
1/2 cup buttermilk
1 Tablespoon unsalted butter, melted
1/2 cup semi-sweet chocolate chips, melted

DRY
2 cups bread flour
2 teaspoons cinnamon
2 teaspoons baking powder
1 1/2 teaspoons baking soda
2 dashes of salt

GLAZE
1 cup confectioner's sugar
1/4 cup of vanilla
1 teaspoon vanilla extract

Again, for the antlers:
Broken mini-pretzels

Oil for Frying
Canola or peanut, about 6 cups

DIRECTIONS

In a large bowl, beat the egg, add the sugar, buttermilk,
butter, and the melted chocolate. In a separate bowl, sift
together the flour, cinnamon, baking powder, baking
soda, and salt. Once that's thoroughly combined, then
slowly add the dry mixture to the wet, adding the white
chocolate chips at the very end. Roll out the dough to 1/4
to 1/2 inch, then use a donut cutter to cut out the rounds
and holes.

Once the oil reaches 375 degrees F, cook the donuts in
batches for two to three minutes per side or until they are
dark brown. Cool them, and then ice them with white
glaze and add melted dots of chocolate, along with the
pretzel antlers.

Makes 8-10 donuts.

THE "WHEN I'M TOO TIRED TO MAKE REAL DONUTS" DONUT

As recipes go, this one doesn't really qualify, but they are still fun to make. We'd been making the basic biscuit dough cutouts for awhile, and then one day I decided to get creative. Splitting them open slightly, I started adding all kinds of fruits to the center, but the ones I liked the best used Craisins. I just love the taste, and they are so easy to make they're fun even when you're too tired to make real donuts!

INGREDIENTS

1 can biscuit dough, your choice
1/4 cup Craisins, raisins, or any of your favorite dried fruit

Oil for Frying
Canola or peanut, about 6 cups

DIRECTIONS

Open the can of dough and separate the biscuits into individual pieces. Pry them apart individually and place a small amount, about 1 tablespoon of dried fruit, on the inside. Then seal the rounds back up by pinching the dough around the edges and they are ready to fry. I don't use a cutter on these; I just fry them as they are.

When the oil reaches 375 degrees F, fry these two at a time, flipping them after two minutes or until the sides are both golden brown. Sometimes they turn over on their own, but don't rely on that. Drain them on paper towels, and then dust them with powdered sugar. These are surprisingly good, and quite easy to make.

Makes as many biscuits as are in the tube, which varies.

If you enjoy Jessica Beck Mysteries and you would like to be notified when the next book is being released, please send your email address to **newreleases@jessicabeckmysteries.net**. Your email address will not be shared, sold, bartered, traded, broadcast, or disclosed in any way. There will be no spam from us, just a friendly reminder when the latest book is being released.

Also, be sure to visit our website at jessicabeckmysteries.net for valuable information about Jessica's books.

Printed in Great Britain
by Amazon